A Cadet's Honor

Mark Mallory's Heroism

Upton Sinclair

A Cadet's Honor: Mark Mallory's Heroism

The present edition is a reproduction of previous publication of this classic work. Minor typographical errors may have been corrected without note; however, for an authentic reading experience the spelling, punctuation, and capitalization have been retained from the original text.

ISBN: 979-8-88830-009-1

CONTENTS

CHAPTER I

A "YEARLING" MEETING

The whole class came to the meeting. There hadn't been such an important meeting at West Point for many a day. The yearling class had been outrageously insulted. The mightiest traditions of the academy had been violated, "trampled beneath the dust," and that by two or three vile and uncivilized "beasts"—"plebes"—new cadets of scarcely a week's experience. And the third class, the yearlings, by inherent right the guardians of West Point's honor, and the hazers of the plebe, had vowed that those plebes must be punished as never had plebes been punished before.

The first and third classes of cadets had gone into summer camp the previous day, immediately after the graduation exercises. From that date, the middle of June to July 1, they have a comparative holiday, with no drills and no duties except guard-mounting, dress parade toward evening, and inspections. And it was during the first of the holiday mornings that the above-mentioned "meeting" was held, beneath the shady trees of Trophy Point, a short distance from the camp.

"I move," shouted a voice in the crowd, "that we elect Bud Smith chairman."

The motion was carried with a shout, and Bud Smith, just out of hospital by the way, was "boosted" up onto one of the guns, which served as the "chair." Bud Smith was a tall, heavily-built youth with a face covered by court-plaster and "contusions," as the results of a West Point fight are officially designated by the hospital surgeon.

"This meeting will please come to order," said the chairman. "And the gentlemen will oblige me by keeping quiet and not compelling me to use my voice much. For I am—er—not feeling very well to-day."

And Bud illustrated his statement by gently mopping his "contusions" with a damp handkerchief.

"We have met," began the chairman, as soon as this formality was over—"we have met, I believe, to consider the cases of three 'beasts,' Powers, Stanard and Mallory, by name (a low groan from the class), and to consider the best method of reducing them to submission. I don't think it is necessary for me to restate the complaints against them, for you are probably all as familiar with the incidents as I. 'Texas' Powers, or as he calls himself, Jeremiah, son o' the Honorable Scrap Powers, o' Hurricane County, Texas, must be disciplined because he fails to understand what is expected of him. He dared to order a superior officer out of his room, and last Monday morning he succeeded in defeating no less than four men in our class—myself among them."

And Cadet Smith again mopped his "contusions," and went on.

"Of course we have got to find somebody to whip him. Then, too, Stanard lost his temper and attacked half a dozen of our class, for no other reason on earth than that they tied him in a sack and carried him out onto the cavalry plain. He, too, was victorious, I am told. And then, last of all, but of all the offenders most insolent and lawless, comes——"

The chairman paused solemnly before he pronounced the name.

"Mark Mallory."

And the storm of hisses and jeers that followed could have been heard at barracks. It was evident that the yearlings had no love for Mark Mallory, whoever Mark Mallory might be.

"Mark Mallory commenced his tricks," the chairman continued, "even before he was a cadet. He was impudent then. And the other day he dared to act as Powers' second. And, worse than all, yesterday, to show how utterly reckless and B. J. he is, he deliberately locked Bull Harris and Baby Edwards up in an icehouse, with the intention of making them absent at taps and compelling them to remain imprisoned all night. It was only by the merest accident, they succeeding in forcing the door, that this plan was frustrated. Now, gentlemen, this thing is about as serious as it can possibly be. Mark Mallory's conduct shows that he's gotten the idea into his head that not only can he avoid being hazed, but even turn the tables upon us and bid us defiance. His attack upon the two cadets was absolutely unprovoked. Bull told me personally that he had not attempted to haze him, and had not even spoken to him. It was a pure case of freshness and nothing else. And he's got to be licked for it until he can't stand up."

Bud Smith finished his speech amid a round of applause, and then fell to soothing his "contusions" again.

It may as well be stated here that Bull Harris' account of the incident that was just now causing so much talk was an absolute falsehood. As told in a previous volume, entitled "Off for West Point," Bull and his gang had made an attempt to lock Mark up, and had failed, and been locked up themselves instead. That was all. But Bull and his gang saw fit to omit that part of the story. It was safe, for no one could gainsay it; Mark's account was not asked for.

"I move, Mr. Chairman," said Corporal Jasper, rising, "that inasmuch as Mallory seems to be the leader of this fool business, that we lick him first, and that, too, to-morrow morning. For it's growing worse every minute. The plebes are getting so downright B. J. that a fellow can't even give an order without fearing to be disobeyed. To-morrow morning, I say. And I call for some one to volunteer."

The young officer's motion took the crowd's fancy.

"Who'll fight him? Who'll fight him?" became the cry, and was followed by a chorus of names offered as suggestions. One was predominant, and seemed to be the most popular.

"Williams! Billy Williams. Get up, Billy! Speech!"

And "Billy" arose from the ground as the cry grew louder, and said that he was "very much honored," and that if the class really selected him he would be most happy to do the best he possibly could.

"Hooray! Billy's going to lick him! 'Ray for Billy."

"I move, Mr. Chairman, that a committee be appointed to convey the challenge on behalf of the class."

"Carried," said the chairman. "I appoint Corporal Jasper and Cadet Spencer. This meeting stands adjourned."

And the yearlings scattered, bearing "Billy Williams" off in triumph.

The committee, much as it hated to, was obliged to delay the sending of the challenge. There were two reasons: In the first place, Mark Mallory, together with the rest of the plebes, was being bullied and tormented just then in the course of a squad drill; and, in the second place, one of the committee, Cadet Spencer, was engaged in doing the bullying, having been appointed "on duty over plebes."

After supper, however, came a blissful half hour of rest to the last-named unfortunates; and then the three yearlings gathered together, took an extra quantity of dignity, and sallied forth to find the three "B. J.'s."

"B. J.," it may be added, is West Point for fresh, and stands for "before June."

Entering barracks, the committee made straight for Mark Mallory's room and knocked.

"Come in, thar!" shouted a voice.

There were four occupants in the room. One was a round, fat-faced boy with an alarmed, nervous look, Cadet Joseph Smith, of Indianapolis, commonly known as "Indian."

In a chair by the window sat a still more curious figure, a lank, bony individual with ill-fitted, straying clothes and a long, sharp face.

Upon his big, bulging knees rested a leather-bound volume labeled "Dana's Geology," and opened at the Tertiary fossiliferous strata of the Hudson River Valley. "Parson" Peter Stanard was too much interested to notice the entrance of the cadets. He was trying to classify a Cyatho phylloid coral which he had just had the luck to find.

Sprawled upon the bed was another tall, slender fellow, his feet hoisted up on the pile of blankets at the foot. All the committee saw of "Texas" Powers was a pair of soles, for Texas didn't care to move.

The fourth party was a handsome, broad-shouldered chap, with curly brown hair. And to him Corporal Jasper, the spokesman, addressed himself.

"Mr. Mallory?" said he.

Mr. Mallory bowed.

"We have come as a committee representing the yearling class."

"I am honored," said Mr. Mallory.

"Pray do not feel so in the least," said Corporal Jasper, witheringly. "The class desires to express, in the first place, its entire displeasure, both as a class and as individuals, at your unprovoked conduct toward two of its members."

"Um," said Mark, thoughtfully. "And did the two members tell you the attack was unprovoked?"

"They did."

"Then I desire to express, in the first place, my entire displeasure, both as a class and as an individual, at being thus grossly misrepresented."

"Bully!" came the voice from behind the mattress.

"In short," continued Mark, "I desire to call the statement of Messrs. Harris and Edwards a downright, unmitigated and contemptible lie."

"Sock it to 'em!" chuckled the voice from the mattress. "Wow!"

"Well put!" added "Parson" Stanard. "Worthy of the great Patrick Henry himself."

"Bless my soul!" chimed Indian, ready to run.

Cadet Jasper took it coolly, like the gentleman he was.

"It is customary, Mr. Mallory," he said, calmly, "for a man to have to earn the right to call a higher class man a liar."

"I am quite ready, sir," responded Mr. Mallory.

"That is fortunate. The class offers you such an opportunity. We are directed to bring a challenge from Cadet Williams, of the third class, to meet him at Fort Clinton at four o'clock to-morrow morning."

"I will consider it a favor," said Mark, politely, "if you will be good enough to inform the class that I am most happy to accept."

"An' look a yere," cried Texas, Mark's chum, raising his head and peering out between his feet. "Look a yere! Whar do I come in, in this bizness?"

"Your seconds?" inquired Jasper, not noticing the interruption.

"Mr. Powers and Mr. Stanard."

"And is there any other information?"

"None."

"Remember, Fort Clinton at four A. M."

"I shall be there without fail. And I thank you for your trouble in the matter."

Cadets Jasper and Spencer bowed and withdrew, while the four "beasts" sat and looked at each other in silence.

"Well," Mark said, at last, "what do you think of it?"

"Think?" growled Texas. "I think it's a skin, that's what I think. An' it's jest like you an' your luck, Mark Mallory!"

And, so saying, Texas kicked the mattress off the bed.

"If you don't do that feller Williams, whoever he is, in the first round, I'll kick you out an' do it myself!"

"But who is this Williams?" inquired Mark, as he picked up the mattress and threw it at Texas. "Does anybody here know?"

"I do," said the "Parson," reverently depositing Dana on the floor. "I do know, and I shall, forsooth, be very happy to tell you about him. Williams is, in the first place, as to physical proportions, the largest man in his class; in the second place, he is the best all-around man— —"

"All round like Indian?" inquired Texas, gravely.

"Inasmuch as," continued the "Parson," "he won a considerable proportion of the Olympic contests, which are celebrated here under the designation of 'the spring games.'"

"That sounds promising," said Mark, thoughtfully. "I wonder if he can fight."

"As to his pugilistic abilities, I am by no means so accurately informed, but if my conjecture be of any value whatsoever, I should be inclined to infer, from the fact that our enemies, the representatives of tyranny and oppression, who are endeavoring to reduce us to submission, have selected him as their champion and representative in arms, that— —"

"He's a beaut," put in Texas, to save time. "And I only wish I'd had Mark's luck."

"And I wish," added the Boston student, "that I could contrive to account for the presence of this Cyathodhylloid fossil in a sandstone of Tertiary origin."

It was not very long after this that "tattoo" sounded. But before it did the little band of rebels up in the barracks had time to swear eternal fealty, and to vow by all that man held dear to be present "at

Fort Clinton at four A. M. to-morrow," there, as the "Parson" classically put it, to fire a shot for freedom that should be heard around the world. Mark swore it, and Indian, too; Texas swore it by the seventeen guns which were stowed away in his trunk, and by the honor of his father, "the Honorable Scrap Powers, o' Hurricane County;" and Peter Stanard swore it by Bunker Hill and, yea, even by Lamachus, he of the Gorgon's crest.

And then the meeting adjourned.

CHAPTER II

MARK'S MYSTERIOUS VISITOR

These were days of work for the plebes at West Point—days of drilling and practicing from sunrise to night, until mind and body were exhausted. And it usually happened that most of the unfortunates were already sound asleep by the time "tattoo" was sounded, that is, unless the unfortunates had been still more unfortunate, unfortunate enough to fall into the clutches of the merciless yearling. When "taps" came half an hour later, meaning lights out and all quiet, there was usually scant need for the round of the watchful "tac," as the tactical officer is designated.

It happened so on this night. The "tac" found all quiet except for the snoring. And, this duty over, the officer made his way to his own home; and after that there was nothing awake except the lonely sentry who marched tirelessly up and down the halls.

The night wore on, the moon rose and shone down in the silent area, making the shadows of the gray stone building stand out dark and black. And the clock on the guardhouse indicated the hour of eleven.

It was not very many minutes more before there was a dark, shadowy form, stealing in by the eastern sally-port, and hugging closely the black shadows of the wall. He paused, whoever it was, when he reached the area, and waited, listening. The sentry's tramp grew clear and then died out again, which meant that the sentry was back in the hallway of the barracks, and then the shadowy form stepped out into the moonlight and ran swiftly and silently across the area and sprang up the steps to the porch of the building; and there he stood and waited again until once more the sentry was far away—then stepped into the doorway and crept softly up the stairs. The strange midnight visitor was evidently some one who knew the place.

He knew just the room he was going to, also, for he wasted not a moment's time, but stole swiftly down the hall, and stopped before one of the doors. It was the room of Cadets Mallory and Powers.

Doors at West Point are never locked; there are no keys. The strange visitor crouched and listened cautiously. A sound of deep and regular breathing came from within, and, hearing it, he softly opened the door, entered and then just as carefully shut it behind him. Having attended to this, he crept to one of the beds. He seemed to know which one he wanted without even looking; it was Mark Mallory's. And then the stranger leaned over and gently touched the occupant.

The occupant was sleeping soundly, for he was tired; the touch had no effect upon him. The visitor tried again, and harder, this time with success. Mark Mallory sat up in alarm.

"Ssh! Don't make a sound," whispered the other. "I've got a message for you. Ssh!"

It is enough to alarm any one to be awakened out of a sound sleep in such a manner, and at such a time, and Mark's heart was thumping furiously.

"Who are you?" he whispered.

The figure made no answer, but crept to the window, instead, where the moonlight was streaming in. And Mark recognized him instantly as one of the small drum orderlies he had seen about the post. Half his alarm subsided then, and he arose and joined the boy at the window.

"Here," said the boy. "Read it."

And so saying, he shoved a note into the other's hand. Mark took it hurriedly, tore it open and read it.

It took him but a moment to do so, and when he finished his face was a picture of amazement and incredulity.

"Who gave you this?" he demanded, angrily.

"Ssh!" whispered the boy, glancing fearfully at the bed where Texas lay. "Ssh! You may wake him. She did."

"Now, look here!" said Mark, in a recklessly loud voice, for he was angry, believing that the boy was lying. "Now, look here! I've been fooled with one letter this way, and I don't mean to be fooled again. If this is a trap of those cadets, as sure as I'm alive, I'll report the matter to the superintendent and have you court-martialed.

Remember! And now I give you a chance to take it back. If you tell me the truth I'll let you go unhurt. Now, once more, who gave you this?"

And Mark looked the trembling boy in the eye; but the boy still clung to his story.

"She did, indeed she did," he protested.

"Where?" asked Mark.

"Down at her house."

"Why were you there?"

"I live there."

Mark stared at the boy for a moment more, and bit his lip in uncertainty. Then he turned away and fell to pacing up and down the room, muttering to himself.

"Yes," he said, "yes, I believe she wrote it. But what on earth can it mean? What on earth can be the matter?"

Then he turned to the boy.

"Do you know what she wants?" he inquired.

"No, sir," whispered the other. "Only she told me to show you the way to her house."

"Is anything the matter?"

"I don't know; but she looked very pale."

And Mark turned away once more and fell to pacing back and forth.

"Shall I go?" he mused. "Shall I go? It's beyond cadet limits. If I'm caught it means court-martial and expulsion. There's the 'blue book' on the mantel staring at me for a warning. By jingo! I don't think I'll risk it!"

He turned to the boy about to refuse the request; and then suddenly came another thought—she knew the danger as well as he! She knew what it meant to go beyond limits, and yet she had sent for him at this strange hour of the night, and for him, too, a comparative stranger. Surely, it must be a desperate matter, a matter in which to fail was sheer cowardice. At the same time with the thought there rose up before him a vision of a certain very sweet and winsome face; and when he spoke to the boy his answer was:

"I'll go."

He stepped to the desk, and wrote hastily on a piece of paper this note to Texas:

"I'll be back in time to fight. Explain later. Trust me.
"Mark."

This he laid on the bureau, and then silently but quickly put on his clothes and stepped to the door with the boy. Mark halted for a moment and glanced about the room to make sure that all was well and that Texas was asleep, and then he softly shut the door and turned to the boy.

"How are we going to get out?" he demanded.

"Come," responded the other, setting the example by creeping along on tiptoe. "Come."

They halted again at the top of the stairway to wait until the sentry had gone down, and then stole down and dodged outside the door just as the latter turned and marched back. Flattened against the wall, they waited breathlessly, while he approached nearer and nearer, and then he halted, wheeled and went on. At the same moment the two crept quickly across the area and vanished in the darkness of the sally port.

"Now," said the drum boy, as they came out on the other side, "here we are. Come on."

Mark turned and followed him swiftly down the road toward Highland Falls, and quiet once more reigned about the post.

There was one thing more that needs to be mentioned. It was a very simple incident, but it was destined to lead to a great deal. It was merely that a gust of wind blew in at the window of the room where Texas slept, and, seizing the sheet of paper upon which Mark had written, lifted it gently up and dropped it softly and silently behind the bureau, whither Mark had thrown the other note.

And that was all.

CHAPTER III

TROUBLE FOR MARK

Time has a way of passing very hurriedly when there is anything going to happen, especially if it be something disagreeable. The hands of the clock had been at half-past eleven when Mark left. It took them almost no time to hurry on to midnight, and not much longer to get to two. And from two it went on to three, and then to half-past. The blackness of the night began to wane, and the sky outside the window to lighten with the first gray streaks of dawn. Not long after this time up in one of the rooms on the second floor of barracks, Division 8, the occupant of one of the rooms began to grow restless. For the occupant had promised himself and others to awaken them. And awaken he did suddenly, and turned over, rubbed his eyes, and sat up.

"Mark! Oh, Mark!" he called, softly. "Git up, thar! It's time to be hustlin'!"

There was no answer, and Texas got up, yawning, and went to the other bed.

"Git up thar, you prize fighter you!"

And as he spoke he aimed a blow at the bed, and the next moment he started back in amazement, for his hand had touched nothing but a mattress, and Texas knew that the bed was empty.

"Wow!" he muttered. "He's gone without me!"

And with this thought in his mind he rushed to his watch to see if he were too late.

No, it was just ten minutes to four, and Texas started hastily to dress, wondering at the same time what on earth could have led Mark to go so early and without his friend.

"That was the goldurndest queer trick I ever did hear of in my life, by jingo!"

It took him but a few short moments to fling his clothes on; and then he stepped quickly across the hall and entered a room on the other side.

"I wonder if that Parson's gone with him," he muttered.

The "Parson" had not, for Texas found him engaged in encasing his long, bony legs in a pair of trousers that would have held a dozen such.

"Are you accoutered for the combat?" he whispered, in a sepulchral tone, sleepily brushing his long black hair from his eyes. "Where is Mark?"

"The fool's gone up there without us!" replied the Texan, angrily.

"Without us!" echoed Stanard, sliding into his pale sea-green socks.

"Bless my soul!" echoed a voice from the bed—Indian was too sleepy to get up. "Bless my soul, what an extraordinary proceeding!"

"Come on," said Texas. "Hurry up."

The "Parson" snatched up his coat and made for the door.

"I think," said he, halting at the door in hesitation. "I think I'll leave my book behind. I'll hardly need it, do you think?"

"Come on!" growled Texas, impatiently. "Hurry up!"

Texas was beginning to get angry, as he thought, over Mark's "fool trick."

The two dodged the sentry without much trouble; it is probable that the sentry didn't want to see them, even if he did. They ran hastily out through the sally port and across the parade ground, Texas, in his impatience, dragging his long-legged companion in tow. They made a long detour and approached Fort Clinton from behind the hotel, in order to avoid the camp. Hearing voices from inside the embankment, Texas sprang hastily forward, scrambled up the bank, and peered down into the inclosure.

"Here they are," called one of the cadets, and then, as he glanced at the two, he added: "But where's Mallory?"

And Texas gazed about him in blank amazement.

"Where is he?" he echoed. "Where is he? Why, ain't he yere?"

It was the cadets' turn to look surprised.

"Here?" echoed Corporal Jasper. "Here! Why, we haven't seen him."

"Hain't seen him!" roared Texas, wild with vexation. "What in thunder!"

"Wasn't he in your room?" inquired somebody.

"No. He was gone! I thought, of course, he'd come out yere."

And Texas fell to pacing up and down inside the fort, chewing at his finger nails and muttering angrily to himself, while the yearlings gathered into a group and speculated what the strange turn in the affair could mean.

"It's ten to one he's flunked," put in Bull Harris, grinning joyfully.

Some such idea was lurking in Texas' mind, too, but it made him mad that any of his enemies should say it.

"If he has," he bellowed, wheeling about angrily and facing the cadet. "If he has it's because you've tricked him again, you ole white-legged scoundrel you!"

Texas doubled up his fists and looked ready to fight right then; Bull Harris opened his mouth to answer, but Jasper interposed:

"That's enough," said he. "We can settle this some other time. The question is now about Mallory. You say, Mr. Powers, you've not the least idea where he is?"

"If I had," responded Texas, "if I had, d'you think I'd be hyar?"

Jasper glanced at his watch. "It's five minutes after now," said he, "and I——"

He got no farther, for Texas started forward on a run.

"I'm a goin' to look fo' him!" he announced. And then he sprang over the embankment and disappeared, while the cadets stood about waiting impatiently, and speculating as to what Mark's conduct could mean. Poor Stanard sat sprawled out on top of the earthworks, where he sat down in amazement and confusion when he discovered that Mark was not on hand; and there he sat yet, too much amazed and confused to move or say anything.

Meanwhile Texas was hurrying back to barracks with all the speed he could command, his mind in a confused state of anxiety and doubt and anger. The position of humiliation in which Mark's conduct had placed him was gall and wormwood to him, and he was fast working himself into a temper of the Texas style.

He rushed upstairs, forgetting that such a thing as a sentry existed. He burst into the room and gazed about him. The place was empty still, and Texas slammed the door and marched downstairs again, and raced back to the fort.

The cadets were still waiting impatiently, for it was a good while after four by this time.

"Find him?" they inquired.

"No, I didn't!" snapped Texas.

"No fight, then," said Jasper. "It's evident he's flunked."

"Wow!" cried Texas! "No fight! What's the matter with me?"

And, suiting the action to the word, he whipped off his coat.

"Not to-day," responded Jasper, with decision. "You'll have your chance another day."

"Unless you run home, too," sneered Harris.

Texas' face was fiery red with anger, and he doubled up his fists and made a leap for the last speaker.

"You coyote!" he roared. "You an' me'll fight now!"

Bull Harris started back, and before Texas could reach him half a dozen cadets interfered. Williams, the would-be defender of his class, seized the half-wild fellow by the shoulders and forced him back.

"Just take it easy," he commanded. "Just take it easy. You'll learn to control yourself before you've been here long."

Texas could do nothing, for he was surrounded completely. Bull Harris was led away, and then the rest of the cadets scattered to steal into camp, but Texas snatched up his coat in a rage, and strode away toward barracks, muttering angrily to himself, the "Parson" following behind in silence. The latter ventured to interpose a remark on the way, and Texas turned upon him angrily.

"Shut up!" he growled. "Mind your business!"

Stanard gazed at him in silence.

"I guess I'll have to knock him down again," he said to himself.

But he didn't, at least, not then; and Texas pranced up to his room and flung himself into a chair, muttering uncomplimentary remarks about Mark and West Point and everything in it. It was just half-past four when he entered, and for fifteen minutes he sat and pounded the floor with his heel in rage. Texas was about as mad as he knew how to be, which was very mad indeed. And then suddenly there was a step in the hall and the door was burst open. Texas turned and looked.

It was Mark!

Texas sprang to his feet in an instant, all his wrath aflame. Mark had come in hurriedly, for he had evidently been running.

"What happened— —" he began, but he got no further.

"You confounded coward!" roared Texas. "Whar did you git the nerve to show yo' face round hyar?"

"Why, Texas?" exclaimed Mark, in amazement.

Texas was prancing up and down the room, his fingers twitching.

"I jest tell you, sah, they ain't no room in my room fo' a coward that sneaks off when he's got a fight. Now I— —"

"I left word for you," said Mark, interrupting him.

"Word for me! Word for me!" howled the other. "You're a—a— a liar, sah!"

Mark's face was as white as a sheet, but he kept his temper.

"Now, Texas," he began again, soothingly. "Now, Texas— —"

"Take that, too, will ye?" sneered Texas. "You're coward enough to swallow that, too, hey? Wonder how much more you'll stand. Try that."

And before Mark could raise his arm the other sprang forward and dealt him a stinging blow upon the face.

Mark stepped back, his whole frame quivering.

"How much?" he repeated, slowly. "Not that."

And then, just as slowly, he took off his coat.

"Fight, hey?" laughed Texas. "Wow! Ready?" he added, flinging his own jacket on the floor and getting his great long arms into motion. "Ready?"

"Yes," said Mark. "I am ready."

And in an instant the other leaped forward, just as he had done at Fort Clinton, except that he omitted the yelling, being indoors with a sentry nearby.

Physically two fighters were never more evenly matched; no one, to look at them, could have picked the winner, for both were giants. But there was a difference apparent before very long. Texas fought in the wild and savage style of the prairie, nip-and-tuck, go-as-you-please; and he was wild with anger. He had swept the yearlings at Fort Clinton before him that way and he thought to do it again. Mark had another style, a style that Texas had never seen. He learned a good deal about it in a very few minutes.

Texas started with a rush, striking right and left with all the power of his arms; and Mark simply stepped to one side and let the wall stop Texas. That made Texas angrier still, if such a thing can be imagined. He turned and made another dash, this time aiming a savage blow at his opponent's head. In it was all the power of the Texan's great right arm, and it was meant to kill. Mark moved his head to one side and let the blow pass, stopping the rush with a firm prod in the other's chest; then he stepped aside and waited for another rush. For he did not want to hurt his excited roommate if he could help it.

A repetition of this had no effect upon Texas, however, except to increase his fury, and Mark found that he was fast getting mad himself. A glancing blow upon the head that brought blood capped the climax, and Mark gritted his teeth and got to work. Texas made another lunge, which Mark dodged, and then, before the former could stop, Mark caught him a crushing blow upon the jaw which made his teeth rattle. Texas staggered back, and Mark followed him up rapidly, planting blow after blow upon the body of his wildly striking opponent. And in a few moments Texas, the invincible Texas, was being rapidly pummeled into submission.

"I'll leave his face alone," thought Mark, as he aimed a blow that half paralyzed the other's right wrist. "For I don't want the cadets to know about this."

And just then he landed an extra hard crack upon the other's chest, and Texas went down in a corner.

"Want any more?" inquired Mark, gravely.

Texas staggered to his feet and made one more rush, only to be promptly laid out again.

"I guess that's enough," thought Mark, as the other lay still and gasped. "I guess that's enough for poor Texas."

And so saying, he took out his handkerchief, wiped the blood from his face, and then opened the door and went out.

"I'm sorry I had to do it," he mused; "sorry as thunder! But he made me. And anyhow, he won't want to fight very soon again."

CHAPTER IV

THE EXPLANATION

Mark had barely reached the head of the stairs before the morning gun sounded, and five minutes later he was in line at roll call with the rest of his class. It is needless to say that Texas was absent.

Texas woke up a while later, and staggered to his feet, feeling carefully of his ribs to make sure they were not really broken. And then he went out and interviewed a sentry in the hall.

"Look a yere, mister," said he. "Where's this yere place they call the hospital?"

The sentry directed him to await the proper hour, and Texas spent the rest of that day, reported by the surgeon as "absent from duty—sick—contusions." And the whole class wondered why.

Mark noticed that the cadets were looking at him at breakfast; and he noticed that the members of his own class were rather distant, but he gritted his teeth and made up his mind to face it out.

"If even Texas called me a coward," he mused, "I can't expect the rest of 'em to do otherwise."

And so it seemed, for that same morning just after breakfast Corporal Jasper and Cadet Spencer paid a visit to Mark.

"The class would like, if you please, Mr. Mallory," said the former, "an explanation of your conduct this morning."

"And I am sorry to say," responded Mark, just as politely, "that I am unable to give it. All I can say is that my conduct, though it may seem strange and mysterious, was unavoidable. If you will allow me, I shall be pleased to meet Mr. Williams to-morrow."

"We cannot allow it," said Jasper, emphatically, "unless you consent to explain your action and can succeed in doing it satisfactorily, which you will pardon me for saying I doubt very much, you stand before the academy branded as a coward."

"Very well," said Mark, "let it be so."

And he turned away, and all through that long, weary morning and the afternoon, too. Cadet Mallory was in Coventry, and not a soul spoke a word to him, except Cadet Spencer, at drill. And he was frigid.

Cadet Powers was released from the hospital "cured" that evening after supper, and he limped upstairs to his room, and sat down to think about himself, and to philosophize upon the vanities of life and the follies of ambition. Mark did not come up until "tattoo" sounded, and so Texas had plenty of time. He felt very meek just then; he wasn't angry any more, and he'd had plenty of time also to think over what a fool he had been in not listening to Mark's explanation of his absence. For Texas had been suddenly convinced that Mark was no coward after all.

While he sat there, a piece of paper sticking out from under the bureau caught his eye. Texas was getting very neat recently under West Point discipline; he picked that paper up, and read as follows:

"I'll be back in time to fight. Explain later. Trust me.

"Mark."

"Oh!" cried Texas, springing up from his chair and wrenching a dilapidated shoulder. "He told me he did that—and I called him a liar!"

Texas walked up and down, and mused some more. Then it occurred to him there might be more paper under that bureau to explain things. He got down, painfully, and fished out another crumpled note. And he read that, too:

"Dear Mr. Mallory: I am in deep trouble, and I need your aid at once. You can tell how serious the trouble is by the fact that I ask you to come to me immediately. If you care to do a generous and helpful act pray do not refuse. Sincerely yours,

"Mary Adams."

Mary Adams was a girl well known to many of the cadets.

The letter was roughly scrawled on a pad, and when Texas

finished reading it he flung it on the floor and went and glared at himself in the mirror.

"You idiot!" he muttered, shaking his fist at himself. "Here them ole cadets went an' fooled Mark Mallory again, an' you—bah!"

Texas was repentant through and through by that time; he grabbed up his cap savagely and made for the door, with a reckless disregard for sore joints. He hobbled downstairs and out of barracks, and caught Mark by the arm just as Mark was coming in.

"Well, Texas?" inquired Mark, smiling.

"Fust place," said Texas, briefly, "want to thank you fo' lickin' me."

"Welcome," said Mark.

"Second place, do it ag'in if I ever lose my temper."

"Welcome," said Mark.

"Third place, I want to 'pologize."

"What's up? What's happened to convince you?"

"Nothin' much," said Texas, "only I been a' findin' out what a fool I am. Hones' now, Mark," and as Mark looked into the other's pleading gray eyes he saw that Texas meant it. "Hones' now, this yere's fust time I ever 'pologized in my life. I'm sorry."

And Mark took him by the hand. They were friends again from that moment.

"I jist saw that second note from Mary Adams upstairs," explained Texas, "an' then I knowed them ole cadets had fooled you that way ag'in. Say, Mark, you're mos' as big a fool as me—mos'."

"That note was genuine," answered Mark. And then as he saw Texas' amazement, he led him aside and explained. "I'll tell you about it," said he, "for I can trust you not to tell. But I can't explain to the rest of the class, and I won't, either, though they may call me a coward if they choose.

"A drummer boy came up here last night—or, rather, this morning. He woke me up and gave me that note, swore it was genuine, too, and I believed him in the end. As you see, Mary Adams wanted to see me, and she was in a desperate hurry about it. Well, I debated over it for a long time; at first I thought I wouldn't, for I was afraid of court-martial; but then as I thought of her in distress I made up my mind to risk it, and I went. As it

21

turned out, old man, you'd have been ashamed of me if I hadn't. There are worse things than being called a coward, and one of em's being a coward.

"I found her in great trouble, as she said. She has a brother, a fellow of about twenty-two, I guess. She lives with her widowed mother, and he takes care of them. I think they are poor. Anyway, this brother had gotten two or three hundred dollars from his employer to take a trip out West. He had fallen in with a rather tough crowd down in the village, and they were busy making him spend it as fast as he could. That was the situation."

"It was tough," commented Texas.

"The problem was to get him away. The girl hadn't a friend on earth to call on, and she happened to think of me. She begged me to try to get him away. And I'll tell you one thing, too, Texas. The cadets say she's a flirt and all that. She may be. I haven't had a chance to find out, and I don't propose to; but a girl that thinks as much of her brother as she does, and does as much for him, is not beyond respect by a good sight. I was really quite taken with her last night."

"Beware the serpent," put in Texas, laughing. "She's pretty, I'm told. Go on."

"Well, I found him, after a couple of hours' search, in a tough dive, with a crowd of loafers hanging on to him. I got him out, but I had to knock down— —"

"Hey!" cried Texas, springing up in excitement. "Had a fight, did ye? Why didn't you take me 'long?"

"I didn't know I was going to fight," said Mark, laughing.

"And did you lick 'em?"

"I only had to lick two, and then the rest ran."

Texas sighed resignedly, and Mark went on:

"I took him home, as I said, and left him with her. I got home just in time for reveille."

"Time to have me call you names and to lick me blue, for the same which I have jest thanked yo," added Texas, his eyes suspiciously moist. "An' look a yere, ole man"—Texas slung his hand around to his hip pocket and "pulled" a beautiful silver-mounted revolver, loaded "to the brim"—"look a yere, Mark. This yere gun, I ain't ever gone out 'thout it fo' ten year. She's a——"

"You don't mean to say you've had it on up here!"

"Sho'," said Texas, "an' I come near usin' it on you, too. Mark, you dunno how a Texas man is with a gun. Mos' of 'em 'ud ruther sell their wives. An' I'm a goin' to give you this to show that—er—that ther' ain't no hard feelin's, you know."

"And I'll take it," said Mark, getting hold of Texas' other hand at the same time—"take it, if it's only to keep you from carrying it. And there aren't any hard feelings."

CHAPTER V

MARK IN DISGRACE

"In my excursions into the various fields of knowledge I have never yet had occasion to investigate the alleged discoveries of phrenological experimentalists, and yet— —"

The speaker paused for a moment, long enough to sigh mournfully. Then he continued:

"And yet I had, I think, sufficient perception of character as delineated by the outlines of physiognomy to recognize at once the fact that the person to whom we refer is in no way a coward."

"I wish I had, Parson," responded his companion, ruefully rubbing a large lump upon his forehead. "I wish I had."

The thin, learned features of the first speaker found it difficult to indicate any amusement, and yet there was the trace of a smile about his mouth as he answered.

"You say he 'licked' you, to use your own rather unclassic phrase?" he inquired.

"Licked me? Wow! He gave me, sah, the very worst lickin' I ever got in my life—which is very natural, seeing that when a feller gits licked down in Texas they bury him afterward. I reckon I'd be a gunnin' fo' him right now, if 'twarn't seein' it's Mark Mallory. Why, man, a feller can't stay mad with Mark Mallory long!"

It was just dinner time and Parson and Texas were sitting on the steps of barracks, waiting for the summons and talking over the events of the previous day.

"And how did this encounter originate?" inquired the Parson.

"All in my foolishness!" growled Texas. "You see yesterday morning when he didn't turn up to fight that 'ere yearling fellow Williams, I thought 'twas cause he was scared. An' so I got mad an' when he did turn up I went fo' him. An' then I went fo' the hospital."

"His conduct did seem unaccountable," rejoined the other. "And yet somehow I had an instinctive intuition, so to speak, that there was an adequate reason. And one is apt to find that such impressions are trustworthy, as, indeed, was most obviously demonstrated and consistently maintained by the German philosopher, Immanuel Kant. Are you acquainted with Kant's antinomies?" the Parson added, anxiously.

"No," said Powers. "I ain't. They ain't got to Texas yit. But I wish I'd had more sense'n to git mad with Mark. I tell you I felt cheap when he did explain. I kain't tell you the reason yit, but you'll know it before long. All I kin say is he went down to Cranston's."

"To Cranston's? I thought we weren't allowed off the grounds."

"We ain't. But he took the risk of expulsion."

"And another, too," put in the Parson, "the risk of being called a coward an' being ostracised by the cadets."

"I dunno 'bout the astercizin' part," said Texas, "but I know they called him a coward, an' I know they cut him dead. There won't even a plebe speak to him, 'cept me an' you an' Injun. An' it's what I call durnation tough now, by Jingo!"

"It don't worry me very much," put in a voice behind them.

The two turned and saw Mark looking at them with an amused expression.

"It don't worry me much," he repeated. "I guess I can stand it if you'll stand by me. And I think pretty soon I can get another chance at Williams, and then — —"

"If ye do," cried the excitable Texan, springing up, "I'll back you to murder him in jist about half a minute."

"It won't be so easy," responded Mark, "for Williams is the best man in his class, and that's saying a great deal. But I'll try it; and in the meantime we'll face out the disgrace. I can stand it, for really there isn't much privation when you have three to keep you company."

"I reckon," put in Texas, after a moment's thought, "I reckon we'll have to put off aformin' o' thet ere new organization we were a-talkin' 'bout. Cuz we kain't git anybody to join ef they won't any of 'em speak to us."

"I guess we three are enough for the present," said Mark, "at least while all the cadets leave us alone. And if they try to haze us I think we can fight about as well as the rest of them. Then there's Indian, too, you know; I don't think he can fight much, but he's—"

"Now, see here!" cried an indignant voice from the doorway, "now see here, you fellows! I think that's real mean, now, indeed I do. Didn't I tell you fellows I was going to learn to fight?" he expostulated. "Didn't I? Bless my soul, now, what more can a man do?"

Mark winked slyly to his companions, and put on his most solemn air.

"Do?" he growled. "You ask what more can a man do? A man might, if he were a man, rise up and prove his prowess and win himself a name. He might gird up his loins and take his sword in his hand and sally forth, to vindicate his honor and the honor of his sworn friends and allies. That is what he might do. And instead what does he do? In slothfulness and cowardice he sits and suffers beneath the rod of tyranny and oppression!"

Mark finished out of breath and red in the face.

"Bless my soul!" cried Indian.

"Such a course is by no means entirely unprecedented," put in Stanard, solemnly. "It is common in the mythology of antiquity and in the legends of mediæval times. Such was the course of Hercules, and thus did Sir Galahad and the Knights of the Round Table."

Poor Joe Smith was gazing at the two speakers in perplexity. He wasn't quite sure whether they were serious or not, but he thought they were, and he was on the verge of promising to go out and kill something, whether a cadet or a grizzly, at once. The only trouble was that the tall, sedate-looking officer of the day, in his spotless uniform of gray and white and gold with a dazzling red sash thrown in, strode out of the guardhouse just then; a moment later came the cry, "New cadets turn out!" and Indian drew a breath of relief at being delivered from his uncomfortable situation.

Saturday afternoon is a holiday at West Point. The luckless plebe, having been drilled and shouted at for a week, gets a much-needed chance to do as he pleases, with the understanding, of course, that he does not happen to fall into the hands of the yearlings. If he does, he does as they please, instead.

Saturday afternoon is also a holiday time for the yearling, too, and he is accustomed to amuse himself with variety shows and concerts, recitations and exhibition drills, continuous performances that are free, given by the "beasts," the "trained animals," or plebes.

It may be well at the start to have a word to say about "hazing" at West Point. Hazing is abolished there, so people say. At any rate, there are stringent measures taken to prevent it. A cadet is forbidden in any way to lay hands upon the plebe; he is forbidden to give any degrading command or exact any menial service; and the penalty for breaking these rules is dismissal. The plebe is called up daily before the tactical officer in charge of his company, and asked if he has any complaint to make.

Such are the methods. The results are supposed to be a complete stopping of "deviling" in all its forms. The actual result has been that when a yearling wants to "lay hands upon the plebe" he does it on the sly—perhaps "yanks" him, as one peculiar form of nocturnal torture is termed. When the yearling wants some work done, instead of "commanding" he "requests," and with the utmost politeness. If he wants his gun cleaned he kindly offers to "show" the plebe how to do it—taking care to see that the showing is done on his own gun and not on the plebe's. And the plebe is not supposed to object. He may, but in that case there are other methods. If he reports anybody he is ostracised—"cut" by every one, his own class included.

This being the case, we come to the events of this particular Saturday afternoon.

> *"There were three wily yearlings*
> *Set out one summer's day*
> *To hunt the plebe so timid*
> *In barracks far away."*

Only in this case there were half a dozen instead of three.

Now, of all the persons selected for torment that year, with the possible exception of Mark and Texas, the two "B. J.'s," Indian was the most prominent. "Indian," as he was now called by the whole corps, was a rara avis among plebes, being an innocent, gullible person who believed implicitly everything that was told him, and could be scared to death by a word. It was Indian that this particular crowd of merry yearlings set out to find.

Mark and Texas, it chanced, had gone out for a walk; "Parson" Stanard had, wandered over to the library building to "ascertain the extent of their geological literature," and to get some information, if possible, about a most interesting question which was just then troubling him.

And poor Joe Smith was all alone in his room, dreading some visitation of evil.

The laughing crowd dashed up the steps and burst into the room. Indian had been told what to do. "Heels together, turn out your toes, hands by your sides, palms to the front, fingers closed, little fingers on the seams of the trousers, head up, chin in, shoulders thrown back, chest out. Here, you! Get that scared look off your face. Whacher 'fraid of. If you don't stop looking scared I'll murder you on the spot!"

And with preliminary introduction the whole crowd got at him at once.

"Can you play the piano? Go ahead, then. What! Haven't got any? Why didn't you bring one? What's the use of being able to play the piano if you haven't a piano? Can you recite? Don't know anything? You look like it. Here, take this paper—it's a song. Learn it now! Why don't you learn it? What do you mean by staring at me instead of at the paper? There, that's right. Now sing the first six verses. Don't know 'em yet? Bah, what will you do when you come to trigonometry with a hundred and fourteen formulas to learn every night? Have you learned to stand on your head yet? What! Didn't I tell you to do it? Who taught you to stand on your feet, anyhow? Why don't you answer me, eh? Let's see you get up on that mantelpiece. Won't hold you? Well, who said it would? What's that got to do with it? No! Don't take that chair. Vault up! There. Now flap your wings. What! Haven't got any? What kind of an angel are you, anyhow? Flap your ears. Let's hear you crow like a hen. Hens don't crow? What do you know about hens, anyway? Were you ever a hen? Well, why weren't you? Were you ever a goose, then? No? Well, you certainly look like it! Why don't you crow when we tell you? What kind of crowing is that—flap your arms, there. Have you got any toothpicks? What! No toothpicks? Don't suppose you have any teeth, either. Oh, so you have toothpicks, have you? Well, why did you say you didn't? Take 'em out of your pockets and row yourself along that mantelpiece with 'em. 'Fraid you'll fall off, eh? Well, we'll put you up again. Humpty Dumpty! Row fast now! Row! Get that grin off your face. How dare you smile at a higher classman! You are the most amazingly presumptuous beast that I ever heard of. Get down now, and don't break any bones about it, either!"

All these amazing orders, rattled off in a breath, and interspersed with a variety of comment and ejaculation, poor Indian obeyed in fear and trembling. He was commanded to fall down, and he fell; he was commanded to fall up, and he protested that the law of gravitation— —"Bah! why don't you get the law repealed?" He wiped off a smile from his terrified face and threw it under the bed. Then, gasping, spluttering, he went under and got it. He strove his very best to go to sleep, amid a variety of suggestions, such as which eyes to shut and which lung to breathe through.

This went on till the ingenuity of the cadets was nearly exhausted. Then one individual, more learned than the rest, chanced to learn the identity of the Indian's name with that of the great Mormon leader. And instantly he elbowed his way to the front.

"Look here, sir, who told you to be a Mormon? You're not a Mormon? Got only one wife, hey? None? Then what sort of a Mormon are you? Why have you got a Mormon's name? Did you steal it? Don't you know who Joseph Smith was? No? Not you, the great Joseph Smith! Suppose you think you're the great Joseph Smith. Well, now, how on earth did you ever manage to get into this academy without knowing who Joseph Smith was? Didn't ask you that, you say? Well, they should have! Fellow-citizens and cadets, did you ever hear of such a thing? There must be some mistake here. The very idea of letting a dunce like that in? Why, I knew who Joseph Smith was about seventy-five years ago. Gentlemen, I move you that we carry this case to the academy board at once. I shall use my influence to have this man expelled. I never heard of such a preposterous outrage in my life! Not know

Joseph Smith! And he's too fat to be a cadet, anyhow. What do you say?"

"Come ahead! Come ahead!" cried the rest of the mob, indignant and solemn.

And almost before the poor Indian could realize what they were doing, or going to do, the whole crowd arose gravely and marched in silence out of the room, bent upon their direful mission of having the Army Board expel Indian because he had never heard of Joseph Smith, the Mormon prophet. And Indian swallowed every bit of it and sat and trembled for his life.

CHAPTER VI

INDIAN'S RE-EXAMINATION

It was a rare opportunity. The six yearlings made for camp on a run, and there an interesting conference was held with a few more choice spirits, the upshot being that the whole crew set out for barracks again in high spirits, and looking forward to a jolly lark.

They entered the building, causing dire fear to several anxious-looking plebes who were peering out of the windows and wondering if this particular marauding party was bound in their direction. It was one of the empty rooms that they entered, however, and there they proceeded to costume one of their number, putting on a huge red sash, some medals, a few shoulder straps borrowed for the occasion, and, last of all, a false mustache. This done, they hastened over to the room where the unfortunate "Mormon" still sat. The "officer" rapped sharply on the door.

"Come in," a voice responded weakly; the cadets came.

"Mr. Smith, sir?" inquired the personage with the mustache.

"Yes, sir," said Indian, meekly, awed by the man's splendor.

"I have been requested by certain of the cadets of the United States Military Academy to investigate the circumstance of your alleged passing at the recent examination. I have been informed by these same gentleman that when questioned by them you exhibited stupidity and ignorance so very gross as to cause them to doubt whether you have any right to call yourself a cadet at all."

Here the cadets shook their heads solemnly and looked very stern indeed.

"Bless my soul!" cried Indian.

"In order to consider these very grave allegations," continued the other, "a special meeting of the Army Board was first convened, with the following result:"

Here the speaker paused, cleared his throat pompously, and drew forth a frightfully official-looking envelope, from which he took a large printed sheet with the West Point seal upon the top.

"United States Military Academy, West Point, June 20th," he read—that is the way all "orders" begin. "Cadet Joseph Smith, of Indianapolis, Indiana, it has just been ascertained, was admitted to the duties of conditional cadet through an error of the examining board. A re-examination of Cadet Smith is hereby ordered to be conducted immediately under the charge of the lord high chief quartermaster of the academy. By order of the Academy Board. Ahem!"

The lord high chief quartermaster finished, and Cadet Smith sank down upon the bed in horror.

"Sir!" shouted the officer, "how dare you sit down in the presence of your superiors? Get up, sir, instantly!"

Indian "got," weak-kneed and trembling.

"The examination will be held," continued the cadet, "in the Observatory Building, at once. Gentlemen, you will conduct Mr. Smith there and await my arrival."

The bogus officer desired time to change his uniform, as he knew it would be risky to cross the parade in his borrowed clothing.

Now the Observatory Building is situated far away from the rest of the academy, upon the hillside near Fort Putnam. And thither the party set out, the cadets freely discussing the probable fate of the unhappy plebe. It was the almost unanimous verdict that one who was so unutterably stupid as never to have heard of the great Joseph Smith would not stand the ghost of a show. All of which was comforting to the listening victim.

The Observatory was deserted and lonely. The door was locked, and the party gained entrance by the windows, which alone was enough to excite one's suspicion. But Indian was too scared to think.

The lord high chief quartermaster presently slipped in, once more bedecked with medals and mustache.

The examining party got to work at once in a very businesslike and solemn manner. The physical examination was to come first, they said. It had been the opinion of the Army Board that Mr. Smith was far too fat to make a presentable cadet. The surgeons were busy that afternoon in trying to piece together several plebes who had been knocked all to pieces by the yearlings for being too "B. J."—this was the explanation of the lord high chief quartermaster—and so it would be necessary to examine Indian here, and at once, too. And if it were found, as, indeed, would most probably be the case, that he was too fat, why then it would be necessary for him to reduce weight immediately.

Several schemes were suggested as to how this might be done. There was the Shylock, the Shakespearian method, of a pound of flesh from near the heart. Cadet Corporal So-and-So suggested that several veal cutlets from the legs—each an inch thick—would serve. A veal cutlet an inch thick he estimated—his great grandfather on his mother's other side had been a butcher, he stated—would weigh three pounds. Then Acting Cadet Sergeant Somebody-Else suggested a Turkish bath, the jockey's method, together with very violent exercise. This plan was adopted finally as being the least likely to be fatal in its results.

But just then somebody suddenly thought of the fact that it would be best to weigh the subject first, which was considered a good idea, but for the fact that they had no scales. This trouble "feazed" the crowd at first. Then the lord high chief quartermaster said that he was a first-rate judge of weight, having slaughtered hogs in his youth, and could tell by the feel. So Mr. Joseph Smith must be immediately "boosted" up and balanced upon the cadet's outstretched hand, there to be shaken and otherwise tested, while the man below made audible calculations by means of trigonometrical formulas as to what was his actual weight.

The result of this experiment, as might have been expected, was by no means very definite. The lord high chief, etc., thought the weight was too much, but he couldn't be sure. And then Cadet "Admiral" Jones proposed another scheme. He had been a juggler "when he was young;" he was used to tossing heavy weights; in fact, he just happened to know that he could throw three hundred pounds exactly twelve feet, the height of the ceiling. It was obvious, therefore, that if Indian weighed over that he would not reach the ceiling; but if he should go through the ceiling that would mean just as clearly that he was under the limit and need not "reduce."

In vain did the frightened boy protest that he weighed only one hundred and fifty; the test must be made, and made it was. Indian's terrified form did not once get near the ceiling, and so reduce he must. The cadets formed a circle about the room.

"Now," said the commanding official, "now you must manage to reduce weight quickly this way, or we shall try the veal cutlet scheme. So you'll find it best to hurry. We want you to run around the outside of this circle. We'll give you just ten and one-quarter minutes by my watch (which runs very fast, by the way) to get around fifty times. And in the course of that you must manage to perspire fifteen pounds of weight (enough to make you go through the ceiling). This is equal to half a gallon of water. Now then! Take off your coat, sir. Ready! Set!! Go!!! Why don't you start, sir? There now! Hurry up! One second—two seconds—three—four—fi'—six—sev'n—eight—nine—ten—'leven! Faster! Faster!! Hurry up! One minute! You haven't lost a pound yet! What! Out of breath already? Faster! That's right! Keep it up now!"

The scene at this stage of the "examination" is left to the imagination; Indian, wild-eyed, panting and red, plunging wildly around in a dizzy circle of a dozen laughing cadets. And in the center the lord high with his watch slowly telling off the minutes.

"Two minutes there, two minutes! Come now, hurry up! Don't begin to lag there! Why don't you stop that panting? There goes the first drop of perspiration. Hooray, there's another! It'll soon be a gallon now. Two and a quarter!"

Poor Joseph kept it up to five, by which time he was so dizzy that he could not stand up; which was the best reason in the world why he sank down utterly breathless in the corner. And there he lay gasping, the cadets in vain trying to get him to rise.

"I think," said the presiding officer, nearly convulsed with laughter—"I think that is reduction enough for the present, and I say we proceed to the 'mental.'"

A conference was held over in one corner of the room, as to what the questions should be; and then in an evil hour (for them) an idea struck one of the cadets.

"See here, fellows," said he. "I think he's been examined enough. Let's get somebody else. Let's get—— Who's that learned chap?"

"Stanard?"

"Oh, yes, Stanard! The Parson! Let's get him."

The idea took with a rush. It would be so much more fun to fool the learned Parson! And in a minute or two half the party, including the lord high chief quartermaster, was on its way back to barracks to hunt up the new victim, while the rest stayed to resuscitate Indian and to write out a list of questions for the "mental examination."

CHAPTER VII

THE EXAMINATION OF THE PARSON

The "examining board" had the good luck to come upon the Parson in a secluded spot near the Observatory. The Parson had left the library for a walk, his beloved Dana under his arm and the cyathophylloid coral in one of his pockets. The "committee" made a rush at him.

"Mr. Stanard?" inquired the lord high, etc.

Mr. Stanard bowed in his grave, serious way, his knees stiff, and his head bobbing in unison with his flying coat tails.

"Mr. Stanard, I have been sent by the Army Board to read the inclosed notice to you. Ahem!"

Mr. Stanard peered at the speaker. His mustache fooled the Parson, and the Parson bowed meekly.

Once more the cadet took out the official envelope and with a preliminary flourish and several "ahems!" began to read:

"United States Military Academy, West Point, June 20th. Cadet Peter Stanard, of Boston, Massachusetts, it has just been ascertained, was admitted to the duties of conditional cadet through an error of the examining board. A re-examination of Cadet Stanard is hereby ordered to be conducted immediately under the charge of the—ahem!—superintendent of ordnance, in the Observatory Building. By order of the Academy Board. Ahem!"

Now, if Cadet Peter Stanard had been a cadet just a little longer he would never have been taken in by that device, for Cadet Peter Stanard was no fool. But as it was, he did not see that the order was absurd.

He went.

Again the procession started with the same comments as before; this time, however, the door was not locked, and the party entered, sought out another room where stood several solemn cadets at attention, respectfully saluting the superintendent of ordnance, ex-lord high.

"Cadet Stanard," said the latter, "take a chair. Here is pencil and paper. What is that book there. Geology? Well, give it to me until afterward. Now, Mr. Stanard, here are ten questions which the board expects you to answer. These are general questions—that is, they are upon no particular subject. The board desires to test your general stock of information, the—ahem!—breadth, so to speak, of your intellectual horizon. Now you will be allowed an hour to answer them. And since I have other duties in the meantime, I shall leave you, trusting to your own honor to use no unfair means. Mr. Stanard, good-day."

Mr. Stanard rose, bobbed his head and coat tails and sat down. The superintendent marched out, the cadets after him. The victim heard a key turn in the door; the Parson glanced at the first question on the paper—

"I. When are cyathophylloid corals to be found in fossiliferous sandstone of Tertiary origin?"

"By the bones of a Megatherium!" cried the Parson, "The very thing I was looking for myself and couldn't find."

And forthwith he seized his pencil, and, without reading further, wrote a ten minutes' discourse upon his own researches in that same line.

"That's the best I can do," said he, wiping his brow. "Now for the next."

"II. Name any undiscovered island in the Pacific Ocean."

The Parson knitted his brows in perplexity and reread the question.

"Undiscovered," he muttered. "Undiscovered! Surely that word is undiscovered. U-m-yes! But if an island is undiscovered how can it have any name? That must be a mistake."

In perplexity, the Parson went on to the next one.

"III. If a dog jumps three feet at a jump, how many jumps will it take him to get across a wall twelve feet wide?"

"IV. In what year did George Washington stop beating his mother?"

A faint light had begun to dawn upon Stanard's mind; his face began to redden with indignation.

"V. What is strategy in warfare? Give an example. If you were out of ammunition and didn't want the enemy to know it, would it be strategy to go right on firing?"

"VI. If three cannibals eat one missionary, how many missionaries will it take to eat the three cannibals?"

"VII. If a plebe's swelled head shrinks at the rate of three inches a day, how many months will it be before it fits his brains?"

And Stanard seized the paper, tore it across the middle and flung it to the floor in disgust. Then he made for the door.

"There's going to be a fight!" he muttered. "I swear it by the Seven Hills of Rome!"

The Parson's blood was boiling with righteous indignation; he had "licked" those same cadets before, or some of them, and he meant to do it again right now. But when he reached the door he halted for a moment to listen to a voice he heard outside.

"I tell you I cannot do it! Bless my soul!"—the Parson recognized the sound. "I tell you I have lost enough weight already. I can't run again. Now, I'll go home first. Bless my soul!"

"Oho!" said the Parson. "So they got poor Indian in this thing, too. Um—this is something to think over."

With his usual meditative manner he turned and took his seat again, carefully pulling up his trousers and moving his coat tails as he did so. Clearing his throat, he began to discuss the case with himself.

"It is obvious, very obvious, that my condition will in no way be ameliorated by creating a suspicion in trying to make a forceful exit through that locked door.

"It would be a more efficacious method, I think, in some way to manage to summon aid. Perhaps it would be well to endeavor to leave in secret."

And with this thought in mind he went to the window.

"It would appear," he said, gravely, as he took in the situation, "that the 'high-thundering, Olympian Zeus' smiles propitiously upon my plan."

And with this classic remark he stuck one long shank out of the window, followed it with another just as long, and stood upon the cornice over the door of the building, which chanced to be in reach. From there he half slid, half tumbled to the ground, arose, arranged his necktie carefully, gazed about him solemnly to hear if any one had seen him, and finally set out at a brisk pace for barracks, taking great, long strides, swinging his great, long arms, and talking sagely to himself in the meanwhile.

"When the other two members of our—ahem!—alliance are made aware of the extraordinary condition of affairs," he muttered, "I think that I am justified in my hypothesis when I say there will be some excitement."

There was.

CHAPTER VIII

THE RESCUE PARTY

Mark and Texas were seated on the steps of barracks when the Parson came through the sally port. The two were listening to the music of the band at the Saturday afternoon hop in the Academy Building, and also watching several cadets paying penalties by marching sedately back and forth in the area.

Stanard strolled in slowly with no signs of excitement. He came up and sat down beside the two in his usual methodical way.

"Good-afternoon, gentlemen," said he. "Good-afternoon. I have something to deliberate upon with you if it is perfectly agreeable."

It was agreeable, and so the Parson told his story, embellishing it with many flourishes, classical allusions and geological metaphors. And when he finished Texas sprang up in excitement.

"Wow!" he cried. "Let's go up thar an' clean out the hull crowd."

"It is best to deliberate, to think over our plan of attack," returned the Parson, calmly, and with a mild rebuke in his tone, which reminded Texas of his promise never to get excited again, made him sit down sheepishly.

"I think," put in Mark, "that we ought to think up some scheme to scare 'em off, or get away with Indian, or something. It's a harmless joke, you know, so what's the use of fighting over it?"

"Oh," growled Texas, in disgust.

"If we could only manage to turn the tables on them," continued Mark. "Shut up a while, and let's think a few minutes."

And then there was silence, deep and impressive, while everybody got his "ratiocinating apparatus," as the Parson called it, to work. Mark was the first to break it.

"Look here, Parson," said he, "what's the name of all those chemicals of yours that you hid up the chimney for fear the cadet officers 'd make you give 'em up?"

The Parson rattled off a list of unpronounceable names, at the mention of one of which Mark sprang up.

"Get it! Get it! you long-legged Boston professor, you!" he shouted. "Never mind why! But I've got something in my pocket that'll—gee whiz! Hurry up!"

The Parson did as he was commanded, and in about as much of a hurry as was possible for him. And Mark tucked the bottle under his coat and the three set off in haste to the rescue, Texas grumbling meanwhile and wanting to know why in thunderation a square stand-up fight wasn't just as good as anything.

An Indian war party could not have made a more stealthy entrance than did the three. They climbed in one of the windows on the lower floor, the basement, and then listened for any sound that might tell them what was going on above. They heard voices conversing in low tones, but no signs of hazing; the reason of that fact being that Indian was just then locked in another room hard at work on his "mental examination," the same one that had been given to Stanard. And poor Indian was striving his best to think of the name of any undiscovered island which he had ever heard of.

Mark took the big bottle from under his coat, set it on the floor and took out the cork. From his pocket he took a paper containing a thick black powder. This he poured carefully into the bottle, put in the cork, and then turned and made a dash for the window. Outside, the three made for the woods nearby and hid to watch.

"Just wait till enough of that dissolves," said Mark. "Just wait."

Meanwhile, upstairs, the hilarious cadets were chuckling merrily over the predicament of their two victims. The lord high, etc., and superintendent had carefully timed the hour that the Parson was to have for his answers; the hour was up, and the official had arisen, turned the key, and was in the very act of opening the door when suddenly—

Bang! a loud report that shook the doors and windows of the building and made the cadets spring up in alarm. They gazed in one another's frightened faces, scarcely knowing what to think. And then up the stairway slowly rolled a dense volume of heavy smoke, that seemed to fill the building in an instant.

"Fire! Fire!" yelled the whole crowd at once, and, forgetting both their victims in the mad excitement, they made a wild dash down the stairs for the door.

"Fire! Fire!" rang out their cries, and a moment later a big bell down at barracks sounded the alarm—"Fire! Fire!"

And over in the woods three conspirators sat and punched one another for joy.

CHAPTER IX

HEROISM OF THE PARSON

The cadets of the academy are organized into a fire department for the safety of the post. It is the duty of the cadets upon the sounding of the alarm—three strokes of the bell, or a long roll on the drum, or three shots, as the case may be—to fall into line immediately and proceed to the scene of the fire. One brigade has charge of a hand engine, another forms a bucket line, etc.

West Point was, of course, thrown into the wildest excitement on the instant that the cry was raised. The cadets poured in from every direction, and in a few moments were on the way at double-quick. Army officers, the soldiers of the regular army at the post, infantry and cavalry, all made for the scene.

The Observatory Building was found to be in imminent peril, apparently; there were no flames in sight, but smoke was pouring from every crevice. Prompt and quick to act, some heroic young cadet leaped up the steps and burst in the door with an ax, though it was not locked and needed only a turn of the knob to open it. The moment an opening was made a cloud of smoke burst forth that drove the party back before it, and at the same instant a cry of horror swelled up from the fast-arriving crowd.

With one accord everybody glanced up to one of the windows on the floor above. There stood a figure, nothing but the head visible in the smoke, a figure of a badly-frightened lad, yelling at the top of his lungs for help! help! help! And the crowd gazed at him in terror. It was Indian, apparently in peril of his life!

Who should save him? Who? The thought was in everybody's mind at the moment, and yet every one hesitated before that barrier of blinding smoke. And then—then suddenly a roar of cheers and shouts swelled up as a hero came to the fore. When every one else trembled this hero alone was bold. He had dashed wildly from the woods, a tall, lanky, long-haired figure. He had fought his way through the craven crowd, his coat tails flying and his long elbows working. He had dashed up the steps, his light green socks twinkling with every stride. And now, while the crowd shouted encouragement, he plunged desperately into the thick of the smoke and was lost to view.

The crowd waited in breathless suspense—one minute—two— and still the imperiled lad stood at the window and the hero did not appear. Could it be that he was lost—overcome by smoke and flame? The throng below hated to think of it and yet—no, there he was! At the doorway again! Had he failed to accomplish his noble purpose? Had he been driven back from the work of rescue? No! No! He had succeeded; he had gotten what he wanted! As he dashed wildly out again the people saw that he carried under his arm a great, leather-bound volume.

"Dana's Geology" was safe!

And a moment or two later somebody put up a ladder and the unfortunate "Mormon" climbed down in haste.

Meanwhile, what of the fire? Encouraged by the example of the "hero," the cadets rushed in to the attack. But, strange to say, though they had hand engines and buckets and ladders, they could find no fire to attack. Several windows having been smashed, most of the smoke had escaped by this time—there had really been but very little of it, anyway, just enough for excitement. There is a saying that where there is smoke there must be flame, and, acting on this rather dubious statement, the gallant fire brigade hunted high and low, searching in every nook and corner of the building, and even searching the desk drawers to see if perchance the cunning fire had run away and hidden there. And still not a sign of flame.

The mystery got more and more interesting; the whole crowd came in—the smoke having all gone by this time—to see if, perchance, a little more diligent search might not aid; and the people kept coming until finally the place was so packed that there was no room for the fire anyway. And so finally every one gave it up in disgust and went home, including the gallant fire brigade. And the three conspirators in the woods went, too, scarcely able to hide their glee.

"It's jest one on them ole cadets!" vowed Texas.

Of course, the Army Board ordered a strict investigation, which was made—and told nothing. All that was found was a few bits of broken glass in one room, and an "examination paper" in another. Indian was hauled up, terrified, to explain; he described his hazing, but steadfastly refused names—which was good West Point etiquette—he vowed he knew nothing about the fire—which was the truth—also West Point etiquette. And since Indian was mum, and there was no one else to investigate, the investigation stopped, and the affair remained a West Point mystery—a mystery to all but three.

CHAPTER X

MORE TROUBLES

"No, sir! I wouldn't think of it, not for a moment. The fellow's a coward, and he don't deserve the chance."

And Cadet Corporal Jasper brought his fist down on the table with a bang.

"No, sir," he repeated. "I wouldn't think of it!"

"But he wants to fight!" exclaimed the other.

"Well, he had a chance once; why didn't he fight then? That's what I want to know, and that's what he won't tell us. And as far as I'm concerned Mallory shall lie in the bed he's made. I wouldn't honor him with another chance."

It was an afternoon late in June, and the two speakers were discussing some ice cream at "the Dutchwoman's" and waiting for the call to quarters before dress parade.

"If that fellow," continued Corporal Jasper, "had any reason on earth for getting up at midnight, dodging sentry and running out of barracks, to stay till reveille, except to avoid fighting you that morning, now, by jingo! I want to know what it is! The class sent me to ask him, and he simply said he wouldn't tell, that's all. His bluff about wanting another chance won't work."

"Well, if we don't," protested Williams, the other man, a tall, finely-built fellow, "if we don't, he'll go right on getting fresh, won't he?"

"No, sir, he won't! We'll find a way to stop him. In the first place, he's been sent to Coventry. Not a man in the academy'll speak to him; he may not mind that for a while, but I think he won't brave it out very long. Just you watch and see."

"The only trouble with that," said Williams, "is that he's not cut by all the fellows. I've seen three of the plebes with him."

"What!" cried the other, in amazement. "Who?"

"Well, there's that fellow he seconded in the fight— —"

"Texas, you mean?"

"Yes, Texas. Then that long-legged scarecrow Stanard was out walking with him this very day. And I saw that goose they call the Indian talking to him at dinner, and before the whole plebe class, too."

"Well, now, by jingo! they'll find it costs something to defy the corps!" exclaimed Jasper. "It's a pretty state of affairs, indeed, if three or four beasts can come up here and run this place as they please. They'll find when an order's given here they'll obey, or else they can chase themselves home in a hurry. That fellow Mallory must be a fool! There's never been a plebe at this academy's dared to do half what he's done."

"That's why I think it would be best to lick him. I'm not sure I can do it, you know, but I think it would be best to try."

"That fellow started out to be B. J. at the very start," growled the excitable corporal, after a moment's thought. "Right at the very start! 'Baby' Edwards was telling me the other day how way last year this fellow met with an accident—fell off the express or something—and while he was staying down at the Falls Baby and a couple of other fellows thought he was a candidate, and started in to haze him. He was sassy as you please then. And after that he went out West, where he lives, and did some extraordinary thing—saved an express, I believe, and sent in an account to a paper for a lot of money. Of course that got him dead stuck on himself, and then he goes and wins a cadetship here and thinks he can run the earth. He was so deucedly B. J. he had to go and lock Edwards and Bull Harris in an icehouse down near the Falls!"

"You see what's happened now," he continued, after a moment's pause. "Your challenge brought him up with a round turn, and he saw his bluff was stopped. He was afraid to fight, and so he hid, that's all. But, by jingo, he'll pay for it if I've got anything to say in the matter!"

And the little corporal made the dishes on the table rattle.

Corporal Jasper and Cadet Williams had finished their council and their ice cream by this time, and arose to go just as the roll of drum was heard from "Camp McPherson." The two strolled off in the direction of the summons, Jasper just as positive and vehement as ever.

"You shan't fight him," he declared. "And if sending him to Coventry doesn't do any good, we'll find some other way, that's all! And we'll keep at him till he learns how to behave himself if it takes the whole summer to do it."

This was the young cadet officer's parting vow, as he turned and entered his tent.

CHAPTER XI

DISADVANTAGES OF "COVENTRY"

"Sir, the parade is formed!"

Thus spoke the cadet adjutant as he approached the lieutenant in command, and a moment later, at the word, the battalion swung around and marched across the campus. It was the evening dress parade of perhaps the best drilled body of troops in the country, and West Point was out in holiday attire to see it.

Seated on the benches beneath the trees on the western edge of the parade ground was a crowd of spectators—visitors at the post and nearly the whole plebe class besides. For this was Saturday afternoon holiday, and the "beasts" had turned out in a body to witness the performance of what they were all hoping some day to be.

It was a "mighty fine" performance, and one that made those same beasts open their eyes with amazement. Spotless and glittering in their uniforms were the cadets, and they went through all manner of difficult evolutions in perfect unison, marching with lines as straight and even as the eye could wish. It is a pretty sight, a mass of gray in a setting of deep green—the trees that encircle the spot, and it made the poor homesick "beasts" take a little interest in life once more.

Among these "beasts" were Mark and Texas. They sat under the trees a little apart from the crowd and watched the scene with interest. Mark had seen dress parades before; Texas had not, and he stared with open eyes and mouth, giving vent to an exclamation of amazement and delight at intervals.

"Look a' yere, Mark," he cried, "d'you think we'll ever be able do that a' way. Honest, now? I think I'll stay!"

"Even after you get through fightin?" laughed Mark.

"I don't think I want to fight any more," growled Texas, looking glum. "Since you an' me fit, somehow fightin' ain't so much fun."

"What's the fun o' fightin' ef you git licked?" he added, after a moment's thought.

"I never tried it," said the other, laughing. "But I suppose you'll be real meek now and let them haze you."

"Yaas!" drawled Texas, grinning. "Yes, I will! Them ole cadets git after me, now, by jingo, I'll go out there an' yank some of 'em out that parade an' lick them all t'once. But say! look at that chap on a horse."

"That chap's the commandant," said Mark, "and he's going to review the parade for a change."

"I wish I was in it," exclaimed Texas, "an' I wish I knew all that rigamarole they're doin' now"—that "rigamarole" being the manual-at-arms. "I jest believe if I had somebody to teach me 'cept that 'ere yellin' tomcat of a Cadet Spencer I'd learn in a jiffy, dog on his boots!"

"There he is now," said Mark, "in the second line there. And there on the outside with his chevrons is Corporal Jasper, 'the committee.' They look very different when they're in line."

"Nothin' 'd make that red-headed, freckle-faced coyote of a drill-master look different," growled Texas. "I jes' wish he was bigger'n me so's I could git up a scrap with him. Jest think o' that little martinet a yellin' at me an' tellin' me I didn't have any sense. To-day, for instance, d'you remember, he was tryin' to show Indian how to march an' move his legs, an' Indian got twisted up into a knot; an' durnation, jist because I laughed, why he rared round an' bucked fo' an hour! What's the harm in laughing, anyhow?"

And Texas glared so savagely at his tormentor as the line swept by just then that Mark concluded there was no harm and laughed.

"You're getting to be very stupid company, Texas," said he. "You never do anything but growl at the cadets. I wish I had some diversion."

And Mark turned away in mock disgust and glanced down the archway of trees.

"Here she comes," he said, after a moment's pause. "That's she walking up the path with a cadet and another girl."

Texas turned as Mark spoke, and looked in the direction of his nod.

"So that's Mary Adams!" he exclaimed. "Well! well! That's the girl you dodged barracks for, and risked your commission, and missed the fight, and got called a coward, and sent to Coventry, and lots else. I swear!"

"That's the one," said Mark, smiling.

"She's stunning pretty," added Texas, as the trio drew near. "Gee-whiz! I don't blame you."

"I liked her right well myself," admitted the other. "That is after I saw her with that brother of hers. She certainly is a good sister to him. But the cadets say she's something of a flirt, and Wicks Merritt advised me to leave her alone, so I guess I shall."

"Sunday school teacher!" said Texas, laughing. "We'll have to call you Parson, instead of Stanard. But I guess you're right. That's not a very beautiful looking cadet she's with."

The three were passing then, and Mark arose.

"I guess I'll have to go speak to her," said he. "She's beckoning to me. Wait a moment."

Texas watched his friend approach the group; he could not hear what was said, however, and so he turned away to watch the parade. By doing it he missed an interesting scene.

Mary Adams welcomed Mark with a look of gratitude and admiration that Mark could not fail to notice. She had not forgotten the magnitude of the service he had done for her. And then she turned to her two companions.

"Miss Webb," she said, "let me present Mr. Mallory."

The other girl bowed, and Mary Adams turned to the cadet.

"Mr. Murray, Mr. Mallory," said she.

And then came the thunderclap. Mark put out his hand; the cadet quietly put his behind his back.

"The cadets of this academy, Miss Adams," said he, "do not speak to Mr. Mallory. Mr. Mallory is a coward!"

It was a trying moment; Mark felt the blood surge to his head, his fingers twitched and his lip quivered. He longed to spring at the fellow's throat and fling him to the ground.

It was a natural impulse. Texas would have done it. But Mark controlled himself by the effort of his life. He clinched his hands behind him and bit his tongue, and when he spoke he was calm and emotionless.

"Miss Adams," he said, "Mr. Murray and I will settle that later."

The two girls stared in amazement, "Mr. Murray" gazed into space, and Mark turned without another word and strode over to where his friend was sitting.

"Texas!" he muttered, gripping him by the shoulder. "Texas, there's going to be a fight."

"Hey!" cried Texas, springing to his feet. "What's that? Whoop!"

CHAPTER XII

THE EMBASSY OF THE PARSON

"What's happened?" cried Texas, as soon as he'd managed to get calm enough to talk coherently. "What's happened?"

"Sit down," said Mark, laughing in spite of himself. "Sit down and stop your dancing. Everybody in the place is staring at you."

Texas sat, and then Mark described to him just what had happened. As might have been expected, he was up in arms in a moment.

"Where is that feller? Now, look a 'yere, Mark, leggo me. Thar he goes! Say, if I don't git him by the neck an'——"

The excitable youth was quieted after some ten minutes' work or so, and immediate danger was over.

"And now," said Mark, "where's the Parson?"

"Over in library," responded the other, "a fossilizin'. What do you want with him?"

"You be good," said Mark, "and I'll let you see. Come on."

They found the Parson as Texas had said, and they managed to separate him from the books and drag him over to barracks. Then Mark, who by this time had recovered his usual easy good-nature, told of "Mr. Murray's" insult again.

"Now, I haven't the least objection," he continued, "of being sent to Coventry. In fact, so long as it means the cadets' leaving me alone, I rather like the idea. But I don't propose to stand a thing like that which just happened for a moment. So there's got to be a fight, and if they won't let me, I'll have to make 'em, that's all."

"Um," said the Parson, looking grave. "Um."

"Now, as for that fellow Murray," added Mark, "I don't propose to fight him."

"Wow!" shouted Texas. "What in thunder do you mean? Now if you don't, by jingo! I'll go and do it myself!"

"Take it easy," said Mark, laughing. "You see, Williams is the man the class has selected to beat me; he's the best fighter. Now, if I beat anybody else it won't do me the least bit of good; they'd still say I'm afraid of Williams. So I'm going to try him first. How's that, Texas?"

"Reckon you're right," admitted Powers, rather sheepishly. "I 'spose you'll let me go and arrange it, hey?"

"I'd as soon think of sending a dynamite bomb," laughed Mark. "You'd be in a fight before he'd said three words. That's what I wanted the Parson for. I think he'd be grave and scholarly even if they ate him."

"Thank you," said the Parson, gravely. "I should try."

"Wow!" growled Texas.

And thus it happened that the Parson set out for "Camp McPherson," a short while later, his learned head full of prize fighting and the methods and practice of diplomacy.

It was rather an unusual thing for a plebe to do—this venturing into "camp;" and the cadets stared at the Parson, wondering what an amount of curiosity he must have to go prospecting within the lines of the enemy. The Parson, however, did not act as if curiosity had brought him; with a businesslike air and a solemn visage he strode down the company street, and, heedless of the cadets who had gathered at the tent doors to see him, halted in front of one before which he saw "Billy" Williams standing.

"Mr. Williams?" said the Parson.

Mr. Williams had been engaged in vigorously drying his face; he paused, and gazed up out of the towel in surprise, and one of his tent mates, Cadet Captain Fischer, ceased unwinding himself from his long red sash and stared.

"My name is Stanard," said the Parson—"Peter Stanard."

"Pleased to meet you," said Williams, stretching out a long, brawny arm.

There was a twinkle in the yearling's eye as he glanced at the skinny white fingers which Stanard put out in return. And, taking in the stranger's lank, scholarly figure, Williams seized the hand and squeezed with all his might.

He expected to hear a howl, but he was disappointed. The Parson drew up his "prehensile muscles," as he called them. The result was that Cadet Williams turned white, but he said nothing about it, and invited the stranger into his tent.

The Parson deposited himself gently in one corner and drew up his long legs under him. Then he gazed out of the tent and said—"ahem!"

"Warm day," said Williams, by way of a starter.

"It is not that the temperature is excessively altitudinous," responded the Parson, "but the presence of a larger proportion of humidity retards perspiratory exudation."

"Er—yes," said Williams. "Yes, I think that's it."

"I have come—ahem!" continued Stanard, "as a representative of Mr. Mallory."

The other bowed.

"Mr. Mallory desires to know—if you will pardon my abruptness in proceeding immediately to the matter in hand—to know if it is not possible for you to fulfill a certain—er—engagement which you had with him."

"I see," said Williams, thoughtfully, and he tapped the floor with his foot for a minute or so.

"Mr. Mallory, of course, understands," he continued at last, "that I have no grudge against him at all."

"Certainly," said the Parson.

"In fact, I rather admire Mr. Mallory, on the whole, though some of his actions have been, I think, imprudent. In this matter I am simply the deputy of the class."

"Exactly," said the Parson, bowing profusely.

"Therefore, I fight when the class says so, and when they say no, what reason have I for fighting? Now, the class thinks that Mr. Mallory has had chance enough, and——"

"But they don't know the circumstances!" protested Stanard, with more suddenness than was usual with him.

"They do not," responded the other. "But they'd like to."

"I do not know them myself," said the Parson. "But I have faith enough in Mr. Mallory to take his word that it was unavoidable."

"You must have a good deal," added Williams, his handsome face looking grave, "a good deal to risk being sent to Coventry."

"I am willing. Examples of yet higher devotion to a fides

amicus, so to speak, are by no means extraordinary. Take the popular instance of Damon and Pythias, or, if you look for one yet more conspicuous, I would mention Prylocates and Tyndarus, in the well-known play of "The Captive," by Plautus, with which you are doubtless familiar."

And the Parson closed his learned discourse with his favorite occupation of wiping his brow.

"The risk is your own," responded the yearling, calmly. "You must not mind if the class resents your view of the case."

There was a few moments' silence after that, during which the Parson racked his head to think what to say next.

"You refuse, then, to fight Mr. Mallory?" he inquired at last.

"Absolutely!" responded the other. "Absolutely, until the class so directs."

Then the Parson drew a long breath, and prepared for the culminating stroke.

"What I say next, Mr. Williams," said he, "you will understand is said with all possible politeness and good feeling, but it must be said. Mr. Mallory has been insulted by some cadets as a coward. He must free himself from the suspicion. Mr. Williams, if a plebe should strike an older cadet, would that make a fight necessary?"

"Most certainly," said Williams, flushing.

"Well, now, suppose he simply threatened to do so," continued Stanard. "Would that be cause enough?"

"It might."

"Well, then, Mr. Williams, Mr. Mallory desires me with all politeness to beg permission to threaten to strike you."

"I see," said the other, smiling at the solemn air with which the lank stranger made this extraordinary request. "I see. I have no objection to his so doing."

"Thank you," said Stanard. "A fight is now necessary, I believe?"

"Er—yes," said Williams. "I believe it is." The fact of the matter was that he saw that Mark was in a position to force a fight if he chose, and the yearling was by no means reluctant, anyhow.

"I thank you for your courtesy," he continued, bowing Stanard out of the tent. "Tell Mr. Mallory that I shall send my second to see him this evening. Good-day."

And Stanard bowed and strode away with joy in his very stride.

"We have met the enemy," was his report to Mark. "We have met the enemy, and there's going to be a fight!"

CHAPTER XIII

PREPARATIONS FOR THE BATTLE

It does not take long for news of so exciting a matter as a really important fight to spread among the corps. No sooner did the Parson leave camp than cadets began to stroll in to find out why he had come, and, learning, they hurried off to discuss the news with their own tentmates. So it happened that by the time the cadets marched down to mess hall to supper every man in the battalion knew that Mark Mallory, the B. J. beast, had succeeded in getting another chance at "Billy" Williams. The plebes knew of it, too. When their rather ragged and scattered company fell in behind the corps at barracks, they were all talking about it, at least when the file closers weren't near. At supper nobody talked of anything else, and everybody in the room was eying Mark and his stalwart opponent and speculating as to what the chances would be.

"Billy'll do him!" vowed the yearlings. "There's nobody in the class that stands more chance."

And the plebes feared it would be that way, too, and yet there were a few at the tables discussing the matter in whispers, venturesome enough to say that perhaps maybe their classmate might win and to wonder what on earth would happen to him if he did.

"It'll mean a revelation if he does!" they cried. "Perhaps it'll even stop hazing."

The mood of the irate little corporal, who had vowed not an hour before that Mallory should not have another chance, may well be imagined.

"I tell you, 'tis a shame!" he vowed to Williams. "A shame! I don't see why in thunder you didn't hold out."

"It's not my fault, Jasper," responded the other, smiling good naturedly. "If you'll think a while, you'll see he was in a position to force a fight at any time he chose. If I refused to 'allow him to threaten to hit me,' as he put it, he could have threatened anyway, and then if that didn't do any good, he'd have actually to hit me, and there you would have been. It's a great deal better this way."

"Yes!" growled Jasper. "That sounds all very well. But look where it puts me, by George! You'll have to get somebody else to arrange it. I won't. I went as a committee and told him he'd not get another chance, and I tell you now I'll not go take it back for anybody, and with that B. J. plebe especially."

"Perhaps he won't be so very B. J. after the fight," responded the other, smiling. "I don't know, of course, but I shall do my best."

"If you don't," said the other, looking serious, "by jingo! we'll be in a thundering fix. There's nobody in the class can beat you, and that plebe'll have a walkover."

This last sentiment of Jasper's was the sentiment of the whole yearling class, and the class was in a state of uncertainty in consequence. Texas was known to have whipped four cadets in one morning, and all of them good men, too; then there was a rumor out that Mark and Texas had had a quarrel and that the latter had gone to the hospital some five minutes later. The two facts put together were enough to make the most confident do some thinking.

It is difficult for one who has never been to West Point to appreciate what this state of affairs meant—because it is hard for him to appreciate the relation which exists between the plebe and the rest of the corps. From the moment of the former's arrival as an alarmed and trembling candidate, it is the especial business of every cadet to teach him that he is the most utterly, entirely and absolutely insignificant individual upon the face of the universe. He is shouted at and ordered, bullied, badgered, tormented, pulled and hauled, drilled and laughed at until he is reduced to the state of mind of a rabbit. If he is "B. J." about it, he is bullied the more; if he shows fight, he has all he wants, and is made meeker still. The result of it all is that he learns to do just as anybody else commands him, and

Never dares to sneeze unless
He's asked you if he might.

All of which is fun for the yearling.

Now, here was Mark Mallory—to say nothing of Texas—who had come up to the Point with an absurd notion of his own dignity, who had outwitted the yearlings at every turn, been sent to Coventry—and didn't care a hang, and now was on the point of trying to "lick" the finest all-around athlete in the whole third class. It was enough to make the corps tremble—the yearlings, at any rate. The first class usually feels too dignified to meddle with such things.

Billy Williams' ambassador put in an appearance on the following Sunday morning, and, to Mark's disgust, he proved to be none other than his old enemy, Bull Harris—sent, by the way, not because Williams so chose, but because Bull himself had asked to be sent.

"Mr. Williams," said he, "says he'll give you another chance to run away."

Mark bowed politely, determined that Harris should get as little chance for insult as possible.

"He'll fight you to-morrow—Fort Clinton, at four, and if you don't come, by thunder! he'll find out why."

Mark's face grew white, but he only bowed again, and swallowed it. And just then came an unexpected interruption.

"Mr. Mallory, as the challenged party, has the right to name the time."

The voice was loud and clear, and seemed to have authority; Harris turned and confronted Cadet First Captain Fischer, in all his glory of chevrons and sword. Now, the first captain is lord of West Point—and Harris didn't dare to say a word, though he was boiling within.

"And, moreover," continued the imposing young officer, angrily, "you should remember that you came, Mr. Harris, as a gentleman and not as a combatant. Mr. Mallory, what is your wish?"

"The time suits me," said Mark, quietly. "Good-day, Mr. Harris."

And Harris left in a very unpleasant mood indeed; he had

meant to have no end of amusement at the expense of Mark's feelings.

"You've a hard row to hoe," said the cadet officer to Mark, "and a hard man to beat. And you were foolish to get into it, but, all the same, I'll see that you have fair play."

"And that," exclaimed Texas to Mark, as he watched the tall, erect figure of the cadet vanish through the sally port. "That is the first decent word I've heard from a cadet since I've been here. Bully for Fischer!"

"It's probable," said Mark, "that he knows Harris as well as we. And now, old fellow," he added, "we've got nothing to do but pass time, and wait—and wait for to-morrow morning!"

Mark slept soundly that night in spite of the excitement. It was Texas who was restless, for Texas had promised to act as alarm clock, and, realizing that not to be on time again would be a calamity indeed, he was up half a dozen times to gaze out of the window toward the eastern sky, watching for the first signs of morning.

While it was yet so dark that he could scarcely see the clock, he routed Mark out of bed.

"Git up thar," he whispered, "git up an' git ready."

Mark "got," and the two dressed hurriedly and crept down the stairs, past the sentry—the sentry was a cadet, and kindly "looked the other way"—and then went out through the sally port to the parade ground. The plain was shrouded in mist and darkness, and the stars still shone, though there was a faint light in the east. The two stole past the camp—where also the sentries were blind— scaled the ramparts, and stood in the center of "old Fort Clinton."

The spot was deserted and silent, but scarcely had the two been there a moment before a head peered over the wall nearest to the camp.

"They're here," whispered a cadet, and sprang over. A dozen others followed him, and in a very few minutes more there were at least thirty of them, excited and eager, waiting for "Billy" to put in an appearance. It was not long before Billy came, and behind him his faithful chum, Jasper, with a bucket of water, and sponges and towels enough for a dozen. About the same time Stanard's long shanks appeared over the breastworks, and Indian tumbled over a moment later. Things were about ready then.

"Let's lose no time," said Jasper, always impatient. "Captain Fischer will act as referee and timekeeper, if it's agreeable."

No one could have suited Mark more, and he said so. Likewise, he stated, through his second, Mr. Powers, that he preferred to fight by rounds, which evidently pleased Mr. Williams. Mr. Williams was by this time stripped to the waist, his suspenders tied about him. And it was evidently as Fischer had said. There was no finer man in his class, and he was trained to perfection. His skin was white and glistening, his shoulders broad and massive, and the muscles on his arms stood out with every motion. His legs were probably as muscular, too, thought Mark, for Williams held the record for the mile. The yearlings' hearts beat higher as they gazed at their champion's determined face.

Mark was a little slower in stepping up; when he did so the watching crowd sized him up carefully, and then there was doubt.

"Oh, gee, but this is going to be a fight!" was the verdict of every one of them.

"Marquis of Queensberry rules," said Fischer, in a low tone. "Both know them?"

Mark nodded.

"Shake hands!"

Mark put out his, by way of answer, and Williams gripped it right heartily.

"Ready?"

And then the simple word "Go."

Let us gaze about a moment at the scene. The ring is surrounded by earthworks, now grass-grown and trodden down, unkept since the Revolutionary days, when West Point was a Gibraltar. Old cannon, caissons and wagon wheels are scattered about inside, together with ramparts and wire chevaux-de-friezes which the cadets are practiced in constructing. In the southwest corner is a small, clear, smooth-trodden space, where the two brawny, white-skinned warriors stand. The cadets are forming a ring about them, for every one is too excited to sit down and keep quiet. The "outlooks," posted for safety, are neglecting their duty recklessly for the same reason, and looking in altogether. Every eye is on the two.

Over in Mark's corner sits Texas, gripping his hands in excitement, wriggling nervously and muttering to himself. Stanard is beside him with "Dana's Geology" as a cushion. The Parson is a picture of calm and scholarly dignity, in direct contrast with our friend Texas, who is on the verge of one of his wild "fits." "Indian" is the fourth and only other plebe present, and Indian is horrified, as usual, and mutters "Bless my soul" at intervals.

On the opposite side of the circle of cadets are Jasper and another second, both breathlessly watching every move. Nearby stands Cadet Captain Fischer, calm and cool, critically watching the play.

CHAPTER XIV

THE AFFAIR AT THE FORT

The two began cautiously, like a pair of skillful generals sending out a skirmish line to test the enemy's strength and resource. This was no such battle as Texas', a wild rush, a few mighty blows, and then victory. Williams was wary as a cat, sparring lightly, and taking no risks, and the other saw the plan and its wisdom.

"Playing easy," muttered the referee, noting the half minute on his watch. "Know their business, it seems."

"Wow!" growled Texas. "What's the good o' this yere baby business? Say, Parson, ain't they never goin' to hit? Whoop!"

This last exclamation was caused by the real beginning of the battle. Williams saw an unguarded face, and quick as thought his heavy arm shot out; the crowd gasped, and Mark saw it. A sudden motion of his head to one side was enough to send the blow past him harmlessly, and a moment later the yearling's forward plunge was checked by an echoing crack upon his ribs. Then for the rest of the round the excited cadets were treated to an exhibition of sparring such as they had never seen in their lives. Feinting, dodging and parrying, the springing pair seemed everywhere at once, and their fists in a thousand places. The crowd was thrilled; even the imperturbable Fischer was moved to exclamation, and Texas in half a minute had seen more skill than his whole experience had shown him in his life.

"Look a thar! Look a thar! He's got him—no—gad! Whoop!"

Texas did as much dancing as the fighters themselves, and more talking than the whole crowd. Captain Fischer had to stop watching him long enough to tell him that the camp, with its sleeping "tacs," was only a few yards away. And then, as Powers subsided, the cadet glanced at his watch, called "Time!" and the two fighters went to their corners, panting.

"What did ye stop for?" inquired Texas, while the Parson set diligently to work at bathing several red spots on his friend's body. "What kind o' fightin' is this yere? Ain't give up, have you? Say, Mark, now go in nex' time an' do him. What's the use o' layin' off?"

"A very superior exhibition of—lend me that court-plaster, please—pugilistic ability," commented the Parson, bustling about like an old hen.

And then a moment later the referee gave the word and they were at it again.

This round there was no delay; both went at it savagely, though warily and skillfully as ever. Blow after blow was planted that seemed fairly to shake the air, driven by all the power that human muscle could give.

"Won't last long at this rate," said the referee, sagely shaking his head. "Give 'em another round—gee!"

Fischer's "gee" was echoed by the yearlings with what would have, but for the nearness of the camp, been a yell of triumph and joy. Williams had seen a chance, and had been a second too quick for Mark; he had landed a crushing blow upon the latter's head, one which made him stagger. Quick to see his chance, the yearling had sprung in, driving his half-dazed opponent backward, landing blow after blow. Texas gasped in horror. The yearlings danced— and then——

"Time!" said the imperturbable Fischer.

Texas sprang forward and led his bewildered friend to a seat; Texas was about ready to cry.

"Old man!" he muttered, "don't let him beat you. Oh! It'll be the death of me. I'll go jump into the river!"

"Steady! Steady!" said the Parson; "we'll be all right in a moment."

Mark said nothing, but as his reeling brain cleared he gritted his teeth.

"Time," said the referee.

And Williams sprang forward to finish the work, encouraged by the enthusiastic approval of his half-wild classmates. He aimed another blow with all his might; Mark dodged; the other tried again, and again the plebe leaped to one side; this repeated again and again was the story of the next minute, and the yearlings clinched their hands in disappointment and rage.

"He's flunking!" cried one of them—Bull Harris—"He's afraid!"

"He's fighting just as he ought," retorted Captain Fischer, "and doing it prettily, too. Good!"

And then once more the crowd settled into an anxious silence to watch.

The story of that minute was the story of ten. Mark had seen that in brute force his adversary was his equal, and that skill, coolness and endurance were to win. He made up his mind on his course, and pursued it, regardless of the jeers of the yearlings and their advice to Billy to "go in and finish him off." Billy went, but he could not reach Mark, and occasionally his ardor would be checked by an unexpected blow which made his classmates groan.

"It's a test of endurance now," observed Fischer, "and Billy ought to win. But the plebe holds well—bully shot, by Jove! Mallory's evidently kept in training. Time!"

That was for the seventh round.

"He's getting madder now," whispered Mark to Stanard, as he sat down to rest. "He wants to finish. If those fellows keep at him much more he'll sail in for a finish—and then, well, I'm pretty fresh yet."

Goaded on by his impatient classmates, Williams did "sail in," the very next round. Mark led him a dance, from corner to corner, dodging, ducking and twisting, the yearling, thinking the victory his, pressing closer and closer and aiming blow after blow.

"Watch out, Billy, watch out," muttered the vigilant Fischer to himself, as he caught the gleam in Mark's eye.

Just then Williams paused, actually exhausted; Mark saw his chest heaving, and, a still surer sign, his lip trembling.

"Now, then!" whispered the Parson at his back, and Mark sprang forward.

The yearling dodged, Mark followed rapidly. There was a moment of vicious striking, and then the cadets gasped to see Williams give way. It was only an inch, but it told the story— Williams was tired. Fischer gazed at his watch and saw that there was yet half a minute, and at the same moment he heard a resounding thump. Mark had planted a heavy blow upon his opponent's chest, he followed almost instantly with another, and the yearlings groaned.

Williams rallied, and made a desperate fight for his life, but at the close of that round he was what a professional reporter would have termed "groggy." He came up weakly at the call.

"Don't be afraid of hitting him," the Parson had said, afraid that Mark's kind-heartedness would incline him to mercy. "There's too much at stake. Win, and win in a hurry"—the Parson forgot to be classical when he was excited.

Obedient to command, Mark set out, though it was evident to him that he had the fight. While Texas muttered and pranced about for joy, Mark dealt his opponent another blow which made him stagger; he caught himself upon one knee, and Mark stepped back and waited for him to rise. And then suddenly a pair of strong arms were flung about the plebe's waist and he felt himself shoved hurriedly along; at the same moment a voice shouted in his ear:

"Run, plebe, run for your life!"

Mark glanced about him in dimly-conscious amazement. He saw that the ring had melted into a number of cadets, skurrying away in every direction at the top of their speed. He heard the words, "a tac! a tac!" and knew the fight had been discovered by an army officer.

A figure dashed up behind Mark and caught him by the arm. It was Fischer.

"Run for your life! Get in barracks!" he cried.

And with that he vanished, and Mark, obeying, rushed across the cavalry plain and was soon lying breathless and exhausted in his room, where the wildly-jubilant Texas joined him a moment later, just as reveille was sounded.

"Victory! Victory!" he shouted. "Wow!"

And by breakfast time that morning every cadet in the corps was discussing the fight. And Mark was the hero of the whole plebe class.

CHAPTER XV

TWO PLEBES IN HOSPITAL

"Say, tell me, did you do him?"

The speaker was a lad with brown, curly hair and a laughing, merry face, at present, however, half covered with a swathing of bandages. He was standing on the steps of the hospital building at West Point, and regarding with anxiety another lad of about the same age, but taller and more sturdily built.

"I don't know that I did him," responded Mark—for the one addressed was he—"I don't know that I can say I did him, but I believe I would have if the fight hadn't been interrupted."

"Bully, b'gee!" cried the other, excitedly slapping his knee and wincing with pain afterward. "Gimme your hand! I'm proud of you, b'gee! My name's Alan Dewey, at your service."

Mark took the proffered hand, smiling at the stranger's joy.

"My success seems to cause you considerable pleasure," he said.

"Yes, b'gee!" exclaimed Dewey, "it does! And to every true and loyal plebe in the academy. You've brought honor to the name of plebe by licking the biggest yearling in the place, b'gee, and that means the end of hazing."

"I'm not so sure of that," said Mark.

"I am," returned the other. "But say, tell me something about the fight. I wanted to come, only I was shut up in hospital. Did Williams put up a good one?"

"Splendid," said Mark.

"He ought to. They say he's champion of his class, and an all-round athlete. But you look as if you could fight some yourself."

"He almost had me beaten once," said Mark. "I thought I was a goner."

"Say, but you're a spunky chap!" remarked Dewey, eying Mark with an admiring expression. "I don't think there's ever been a plebe dared to do half what you've done. The whole class is talking about you."

"Is that so?" inquired Mark, laughing. "I didn't mean to do anything reckless."

"What's the difference," laughed the other, "when you can lick 'em all, b'gee? I wish I could do it," he added, rather more solemnly. "Then, perhaps, maybe I wouldn't be the physical wreck that I am."

"You been fighting, too?" inquired Mark, laughing.

"Betcher life, b'gee!" responded the other, emphatically. "Only I wasn't as clever at it as you."

"Tell me about it," said Mark, with interest.

"It happened last Saturday afternoon, and I've been in hospital ever since, b'gee. Some of the cadets caught me taking a walk up somewhere near what they call 'Crow's Nest.' And so they set out to have some fun. Told me to climb a tree, in the first place. I looked at the tree, and, b'gee, there wasn't a limb for thirty feet, and the limbs there were rotten. There was one of 'em, a big, burly fellow with short hair and a scar on his cheek——"

"Bull Harris!" cried Mark.

"Yes," said Dewey, "that's what they called him—'Bull.'"

"Did you fight with him?"

"Betcher life, b'gee! He tried to make me climb that tree, and, b'gee, says I, 'I won't, b'gee!' Then I lammed him one in the eye——"

"Bully!" cried Mark, and then he added, "b'gee!" by way of company. "Did he beat you?"

"Betcher life," cried the other. "That is, the six of 'em did."

"You don't mean to say the crowd attacked you?"

"That's what I said."

"Well, sir!" exclaimed Mark, "the more I hear of that Bull Harris the bigger coward I find him. It's comforting to know that all the cadets aren't that way."

"Very comforting!" responded the other, feeling of the bandage on his swollen jaw. "Very comforting! Reminds me of a story I heard once, b'gee, of a man who got a thousand dollars' comfort from a railroad for having his head cut off."

Mark laughed for a moment, and then he fell to tapping the step thoughtfully with his heel. He was thinking over a plan.

"I don't suppose you've much love for the yearlings," he remarked, at last.

"Bet cher life not," laughed the other. "I've about as much as a mother-in-law for a professional joke writer, b'gee! Reminds me of a story I once heard—but go on; I want to hear what you had to say. Tell my story later."

"Well, three friends of mine have formed a sort of an informal alliance for self-defence——"

"Bully, b'gee!" cried Dewey, excitedly.

"And I thought maybe you'd like to——"

"Join? Bet cher life, b'gee! Why didn't you say so before? Whoop!"

And thus it happened that Member Number Five of the West Point "alliance" was discovered.

"I don't think this famous alliance is going to have much to do at the start," said Mark, as soon as Master Dewey had recovered from his excitement, "for I rather fancy the yearlings will leave us alone for a time."

"Bet cher life, b'gee!" assented the other. "If they don't look out they won't have time to be sorry."

"B'gee!" added Mark, smiling.

"Do I say that much?" inquired the other, with a laugh. "I suppose I must, because the fellows have nicknamed me 'B'gee.' I declare I'm not conscious of saying it. Do I?"

"Bet cher life, b'gee," responded Mark, whereupon his new acquaintance broke into one of his merry laughs.

"Let's go around to barracks," said Mark, finally—it was then just after breakfast time. "I expect they'll want me to report for drill. I thought I'd get off for the morning on the strength of my 'contusions,' as they call them. But the old surgeon was too sly for me. He patched me up in a jiffy."

"What was the matter with you?" inquired Dewey, dropping his smile.

"One eye's about half shut, as you see," responded Mark, "and then I had quite a little cut on the side of my head where Williams hit me once. Otherwise I am all right—only just a little rocky."

"As the sea captain remarked of the harbor, b'gee," added the other. "But tell me, how's Williams?"

"Pretty well done up, as the laundryman remarked, to borrow

your style of illustration," Mark responded, laughing. "They had to carry poor Williams down here. He's in there now being fixed up. And say, you should have seen how queerly the surgeon looked at us two. He knew right away what was up, of course, but he never said a word—just entered us 'sick—contusions.' Is that what you were?"

"Bet cher life, b'gee!" responded the other. "But he tried to get me to tell what was up. He rather suspected hazing, I think. I didn't say anything, though."

"It would have served some of those chaps just right if you had," vowed Mark. "You know you could have every one of them expelled."

The two had reached the area of barracks by this time, and hurried over to reach their rooms before inspection.

"And don't you mention what I've told you about this great alliance to a soul," Mark enjoined. "We'd have the whole academy about our ears in a day."

Dewey assented.

"What's the name of it?" he inquired.

"Haven't got any name for it yet," said Mark, "or any leader either, in fact. We're waiting to get a few more members, enough for a little excitement. Then we'll organize, elect a leader, swear allegiance, and you can bet there'll be fun—b'gee!"

"Come up to my room," he added, after a moment's pause, "as soon as you get fixed up for inspection, and I'll introduce you to the other fellows."

With which parting word he turned and bounded up the stairs to his own room.

CHAPTER XVI

THE PARSON'S INDIGNATION

Mark found his roommate and faithful second, Texas, busily occupied in cleaning up for the morning inspection. Texas wasn't looking for Mark; it had been Texas' private opinion that Mark had earned a week's holiday by the battle of the morning, and that the surgeon would surely grant it. When Mark did turn up, however, Texas wasted no time in complaining of the injustice, but got his friend by the hand in a hurry.

"Ole man," he cried, "I'm proud of you! I ain't had a chance to say how proud I am!"

"Thanks," said Mark, laughing, "but look out for that sore thumb—and for mercy's sakes don't slap me on that shoulder again. I'm more delicate than I look. And say, Texas, I've got a new member for our secret society—b'gee!"

Texas looked interested.

"He's a pretty game youngster," Mark continued, "for when Bull Harris and that gang of his tried to haze him, he sailed in and tried to do the crowd."

"Oh!" cried Texas, excitedly. "Wow! I wish I'd 'a' been there. Say, Mark, d'ye know I've been a missin' no end o' fun that a'way. Parson had a fight, an' I didn't see it; you had one daown to Cranston's, an' I missed that; an' yere's another!"

Texas looked disgusted and Mark burst out laughing.

"'Tain't any fun," growled the former. "But go on, tell me 'bout this chap. What does he look like?"

"He's not as tall as we," replied Mark, "but he's very good-looking and jolly. And when he says "B'gee" and laughs, you can't help laughing with him. Hello, there's inspection!"

This last remark was prompted by a sharp rap upon the door. The two sprang up and stood at attention. "Heels together, eyes to the front, chest out"—they knew the whole formula by this time. And Cadet Corporal Jasper strode in, found fault with a few things and then went on to carry death and devastation into the next place.

A few minutes later the Parson strolled in.

"Yea, by Zeus," began he, without waiting for the formality of a salutation. "Yea, by Apollo, the far-darting, this is indeed an outrage worthy of the great Achilles to avenge. And I do swear by the bones of my ancestors, by the hounds of Diana, forsooth even by Jupiter lapis and the Gemini, that never while I inspire the atmosphere of existence will I submit myself to so outrageous an imposition——"

"Wow!" cried Texas. "What's up?"

"Sit down and tell us about it," added Mark.

"It is written in the most immortal document," continued the Parson, without noticing the interruption, "that ever emanated from the mind of man, the Declaration of Independence (signed, by the way, by an ancestor of my stepmother), that among the inalienable privileges of man, co-ordinate with life and liberty itself, is the pursuit of happiness. And in the name of the Seven Gates of Thebes and the Seven Hills of the Eternal City, I demand to know what happiness a man can have if all his happiness is taken from him!"

"B'gee! Reminds me of a story I heard about a boy who wanted to see the cow jump over the moon on a night when there wasn't any moon, b'gee."

Mark and Texas looked up in surprise and the Parson faced about in obvious displeasure at the interruption.

"In the name of all the Olympian divinities and the inhabitants of Charon and the Styx," he cried, angrily, "I demand to know——"

"Come in," said Mark, laughing. "Excuse me for interrupting, Parson, but this is Mr. Alan Dewey, b'gee, member Number Five of our band of desperate buccaneers, if you please. Mr. Dewey, allow me to introduce you to the gentleman who 'reminded' you of that last story, Mr. Peter Stanard, of Boston, Massachusetts, the cradle of liberty, the nurse of freedom, and the center and metropolis of the geological universe."

The Parson bowed gravely.

"While I am, together with all true Bostonians, proud of the reputation which my city has merited, yet I am——"

"Also to Mr. Jeremiah Powers," continued Mark, cutting the Parson off in his peroration.

"Son o' the Honorable Scrap Powers, o' Hurricane County, Texas," added Texas, himself.

Young Dewey shook hands all around, and then sat down on the bed, looking at Mark with a puzzled expression on his face, as much as to say, "what on earth have I struck—b'gee?" Mark saw his expression and undertook to inform him, making haste to start before the Parson could begin again on the relative merits of Boston and the rest of the civilized universe.

"Powers and Stanard," said he, "are the members of our organization, together with Indian, the fat boy."

"I see," said Dewey, at the same time thinking what a novel organization it must be. "There's Indian now."

Indian's round, scared face peered in through the open doorway just then. He was introduced to Number Five, whereupon Number Five remarked 'Very pleased to meet you, b'gee.' And Indian echoed 'Bless my soul!' and crept into the room and sat down in an inconspicuous corner.

There was a moment's pause and then the Parson commenced:

"If I remember correctly, we were occupied when last interrupted, by—ahem! a rather facetious observation upon the subject of our solitary lunar satellite and quadruped of the genus Bos—occupied I say in considering the position which the metropolis of Boston has obtained——"

"Drop Boston!" laughed Mark. "We weren't on Boston anyhow. Boston came in afterward—as Boston always does, in fact."

"Which reminds me, b'gee," put in the newcomer, "of a story I once heard of——"

"Drop the story, too!" exclaimed Mark. "I want to know what the Parson was so indignant about."

"Yes, yes!" put in Texas. "That's what I say, too. And be quick about it. We've only ten minutes 'fore drill, an' if there's anybody got to be licked, why, we got to hustle."

"Well," said Stanard, drawing a long breath. "Well! Since it is the obvious and, in fact, natural desire of the company assembled, so expressed by them, that I should immediately proceed to a summary and concise statement of the matter in hand, pausing for no extensive introductions or formal perorations, but endeavoring assiduously to impart to my promulgations a certain clarified conciseness which in matters of this peculiar nature is so eminently advantageous——"

The Parson was interrupted at this place by a subdued "B'gee!" from Dewey, followed by a more emphatic "Wow!" and a scarcely audible "Bless my soul!"

"What's the matter?" he inquired, stopping short and looking puzzled.

"Nothing," replied Mark. "I didn't say anything."

"Oh!" said the Parson. "Excuse me. Where was I? Oh, yes, I was just saying I would be brief. Gentlemen—ahem!—when I entered this room I was in a condition of violent anger. As I stated, an outrage had been offered me such as neither Parmenides, nor Socrates, nor even Zeno, stoic of stoics, could have borne. And I have resolved to seek once more, as a prodigal son, the land of my birth, where science is fostered instead of being repressed as in this hotbed of prejudice and ignorance. I——"

"What's up?" cried the four.

"I am coming to that," said the Parson, gravely, stretching out his long shanks, drawing up his trousers, and displaying his sea-green socks. "This same morning—and my friend Indian will substantiate my statement, for he was there—a low, ignorant cadet corporal did enter into my room, for inspection, by Zeus, and after generally displaying his ill-manners, he turned to me and conveyed the extraordinary information that, according to rules, forsooth, I must be deprived of the dearest object of my affections, solace of my weary hours, my friend in time of need, my companion in sickness, which through all the trials of adversity has stuck to me closer than a brother, my only joy, my——"

"What?" cried the four, by this time wrought up to the highest pitch of indignation and excitement.

"My one refuge from the cares of life," continued the solemn Parson, "the one mitigating circumstance in this life of tribulation, the only——"

"What? What? What?"

"What? Of all things what, but this? What but my life, my pride, my hope—my beloved volume of 'Dana's Geology,' friend of my——"

And the roar of laughter which came then made the sentry out on the street jump in alarm. The laughing lasted until the cry came:

"New cadets turn out!" which meant drill; and it lasted after that, too, so that Cadet Spencer, drillmaster, "on duty over plebes," spent the next hour or two in wondering what on earth his charges kept snickering at. Poor Texas was the subject of a ten-minute discourse upon "impertinence and presumption," because he was guilty of the heinous offense of bursting out laughing in the midst of one of the irate little drillmaster's tirades.

CHAPTER XVII

INDIAN IN TROUBLE

What manner of torture is squad drill has already been shown; and so the reader should have some idea of what our five friends were going through. Squad drill lasts for the first two weeks or so of plebe life—that is, before the move into camp. The luckless victims begin after breakfast, and at regular (and frequent) periods until night are turned out under the charge of some irascible yearling to be taught all manner of military maneuvers—setting up drill, how to stand, to face, and, in fact, how to walk.

Most people, those who have not been to West Point, are under the delusion that they know how to walk already. It usually takes the luckless plebe a week to get that idea hammered out of his head, and another week besides to learn the correct method. The young instructor, presenting, by the way, a ludicrous contrast in his shining uniform of gray and white and gold, with his three or four nervous and variously costumed pupils, takes the bayonet of his gun for a drill stick and marches "his" squad over into a secluded corner of the area and thus begins the above-mentioned instructions:

"At the word forward, throw the weight of the body upon the right leg, the left knee straight. At the word march, move the left leg smartly without jerk, carry the left foot forward thirty inches from the right, the sole near the ground, the toe a little depressed, knee straight and slightly turned out. At the same time throw the weight of the body forward (eyes to the front) and plant the foot without shock, weight of the body resting upon it; next, in like manner, advance the right foot and plant it as above. Continue to advance without crossing the legs or striking one against the other, keeping the face direct to the front. Now, forward, common time, march. Depress the toe so that it strikes the ground at the same time as the heel (palms of the hands squarely to the front. Head up)"—and so on.

That is the way the marching exercise goes, exclusive, of course, of all interruptions, comments and witticisms on the instructor's part. The plebe begins to get used to it after the first week or so, when the stiffness rubs off, and then a certain amount of rivalry begins to spring up among various squads, and everybody settles down to the business of learning. The squads are consolidated later on, and gradually the class is merged into one company. Such as they are, these drills, together with inspections, meals and "rests" (with hazing), occupy almost the entire time of the two weeks in barracks.

And now for our five "rebels."

That particular Monday morning the plebes had an hour's rest before dinner, in which to do as they pleased (or as the yearlings pleased). And during this hour it was that one of "the five," the always luckless and unhappy one, got into trouble. The one was Indian, or the Mormon. Indian, it seemed, was always thought of whenever there was any deviling to be done. The other plebes did as they were told, and furnished amusement on demand, but they always realized that it was all in fun. Indian, however, was an innocent, gullible youth, who took everything solemnly, and was in terror of his unhappy life every moment of the day. And he was especially unfortunate this time because he fell into the hands of "Bull" Harris and his gang.

It is not the intention of the writer to give the impression that all cadets at West Point were or are like "Bull" Harris, or that hazing of his peculiar variety is an everyday affair. But it would be hard to find one hundred men without a cowardly, cruel nature among them. "Bull" Harris and his crowd represented the lower element of the yearling class, and made hazing their business and diversion. They were the especial dread of the plebes in consequence. Bull had tried his tricks upon Mark to his discomfort, and ever since that had left Mark strictly alone, and confined his efforts to less vigorous victims, among which were Dewey, and now Indian.

Indian had selected a rather grewsome occupation, anyhow, at the particular moment when he was caught. It was just in keeping with the peculiarly dejected frame of mind he was in (after squad drill). He was wandering through the graveyard, which is situated in a lonely portion of the post, way off in the northwestern corner. Some heroes, West Point's bravest, lie buried there, and Indian was dejectedly wondering if those same heroes would ever have stuck through plebe days in barracks if they had had a drill master like that "red-headed coyote," Chick Spencer. He had about concluded they would not have, when he heard some muffled laughter and the sound of running feet. A moment later the terrified plebe found himself completely surrounded by a dozen merry yearlings, out for a lark. Prominent among them were Bull and his toadying little friend, Baby Edwards.

It is correct West Point etiquette for a plebe, when "captured" to go meekly wherever desired. Indian went, and the party disappeared quickly in the woods on one side, the captive being hidden completely in the circle of cadets.

There was one person who had seen him, however, and that one person was the Parson, who had been about to enter the gate to join his friend. And the Parson, when he saw it, turned quickly on his heel and strode away back to barracks as fast as his long legs could carry him without loss of scholarly dignity.

"Yes, by Zeus," he muttered to himself. "Yea, by Zeus, the enemy is fierce upon our trail. And swiftly, forsooth, will I hie me to my companions and inform them of this insufferable indignity."

All unconscious of the learned gentleman's discovery, the yearlings meanwhile were hurrying away into a secluded portion of the woods; for they knew that their time was short, and that they would have to make haste. The terrified victim was pushed over logs and through brambles until he was almost exhausted, the captors meanwhile dropping dire hints as to his fate.

"An Indian he is!" muttered Bull Harris. "An Indian!" (The plebe was as red as one then.) "He shall die an Indian's death!"

"That's what he shall!" echoed the crowd. "An Indian! An Indian! We'll burn him at the stake!"

"He, he! the only good Indian's a dead Indian, he, he!" chimed in Baby, chuckling at his own witticism. "He, he!"

All this poor Joseph did not fail to notice, and as was his habit, he believed every word of it. Nor did his mind regain any of its composure as the procession continued its solemn marching through the lonely woods, to the tune of the yearlings' cheerful remarks. The latter were chuckling merrily to themselves, but when they were in hearing of their victim their tone was deep and awful, and their looks dark and savage. Poor Indian's fat, round eyes stared wider and rounder every minute; his equally round, red face grew redder, and his gasping exclamations more frequent and violent.

"Bless my soul!" he cried, "what extraordinary proceedings!"

"Ha! ha!" muttered the yearlings. "See, he trembles! Behold how the victim pales!"

A short distance farther in the woods the party came upon a small clearing.

"Just the spot!" cried Bull. "See the tree in the center. That is the stake, and to that we will tie him, while the smoke ascends to the clouds of heaven."

"Just the spot!" echoed Baby, chuckling gleefully.

"It is quiet," continued Bull, in a low, sepulchral tone. "Yes, and his cries of agony will be heard by none. Advance, wretched victim, and prepare to die the death which your savage ancestors did inflict upon our fathers. Advance!"

"Advance!" growled the crowd.

"Bless my soul!" cried the Indian.

He was no more capable of advancing than he was of flying. His knees were shaking in violent terror. Great beads of perspiration rolled from the dimples in his fat little cheeks. Limp and helpless, he would have sunk to the ground, but for the support of his captors.

"Advance!" cried Bull, again, stamping on the ground in mock impatience and rage. "Bodyguard, bring forth the wretch!"

In response to this order several of the cadets dragged the unhappy plebe to the tree and held him fast against it. Bull Harris produced from under his coat a coil of rope, and Indian felt it being wrapped about his body.

Up to this point he had been silent from sheer terror; but the feeling of the rough rope served to bring before him with startling reality the awfulness of the fate that was in store for him. He opened his mouth and forthwith gave vent to a cry so weird and unearthly that the yearlings burst out into a shout of laughter. It was no articulate cry, simply a wild howl. It rang and echoed through the woods, like the hoot of an owl at night, or the strange, half-human cry of a frightened dog. And it died into a gasp that Bull Harris described as "the sigh of a homesick bullfrog."

Indian's musical efforts continued as the horrible rope was wound about his body. Each wail was louder and more unearthly, more mirth-provoking to the unpitying cadets, until at last, when Bull Harris finished and stepped back to survey his work, the frightened plebe could be likened to nothing less than a steam calliope.

The yearlings were so much amused by his powers that they resolved forthwith that the show must not stop. And so, without giving the performer chance to breathe even, they set to work diligently collecting sticks and leaves.

"Heap 'em up! Heap 'em up!" cried Bull. "Heap 'em up! And soon shall the fire blaze merrily."

Naturally, since Indian's shrieks and howls continued unabated in quantity or variety through all this, the yearlings were in no hurry to finish, but took care to prolong the agony, sport as they called it, as long as possible. So, while the red-faced, perspiring victim panted, grunted, howled, and wriggled, they piled the wood about him with exasperating slowness, rearranging, inspecting, and discussing the probable effect of each and every stick of wood they laid on.

It was done, at last, however, and the result was a great pile of fagots surrounding and half covering the unfortunate lad. They were fagots selected as being the driest that could be found in the dry and sun-parched clearing. There was a moment or two later on when Bull wished they had not been quite so dry, after all.

The crowd stood and admired their work for a few moments longer, while Indian's weird wails rose higher than ever. Then Bull stepped forward.

"Art thou prepared to die?" he inquired in his most sepulchral tone.

Indian responded with a crescendo in C minor.

"He answereth not!" muttered the other. "Let him scorn our

questions who dares. What, ho! Bring forth the torch! We shall roast him brown."

"And when he is brown," roared another, "then he will cease to be Smith!"

"Yes," cried Bull, "for he will be dead. His bones shall bleach on the plains. On his flesh we will make a meal!"

"An Indian meal!" added Baby, chuckling merrily over his own joke.

"Several meals," continued Bull, solemnly. "There is enough of him for a whole table d'hote. How about that? Aren't you?"

"Wow! Wo-oo-oo-oooo!" wailed Indian.

"He mocks us!" cried the spokesman. "He scorns to answer. Very well! We shall see. Is the torch lit?"

The torch, an ordinary sulphur match, was not lit. But Bull produced one from the same place as the rope and held it poised. He waited a moment while the yearlings discussed the next action.

"I say we let him loose," said one. "He's scared enough."

"Nonsense!" laughed Bull, "I'm not going to stop yet. I'm going to set him afire."

"Set him afire!" echoed the crowd, in a whisper.

"'Sh! Yes," responded the other. "Not really, you know, but just enough to scare him. We'll set fire to the wood and then when it's begun to smoke some we'll put it out."

"That's risky," objected somebody. "I say we— —"

"Nonsense!" interrupted the leader. "If you don't want to, run home. I am."

And so once more he turned toward the wretched captive, who still kept up his shrieks.

"Ha, ha!" he muttered, "thy time has come. Say thy last prayer."

With which words he stepped quickly forward, struck the match upon his heel, and after holding it for a moment knelt down before the pile of leaves and wood.

"Wow! Wow!" roared Indian. "Stop! Stop! Help! Wo-oo-oo!"

Another of those steam calliope wails.

"He shrieks for mercy!" muttered Bull. "He shrieks in vain. There!"

The last exclamation came as he touched the match to the leaves, stood up and worked off to join his companions.

"Form a ring," he said, "and dance about him as he dies."

The terror of Indian can scarcely be imagined; he was almost on the verge of fainting as the hot choking smoke curled up and around his face. His yells grew louder and increased to a perfect shriek of agony.

"Don't you think we'd better stop it now?" inquired one of the yearlings, more timid than the rest.

"Rats!" laughed Bull. "It's hardly started. I'll manage it."

Bull's "management" proved rather untrustworthy; for Bull had forgotten to take into account the dryness of the twigs, and also another factor. The air had been still as he struck the match, but just at that moment a slight breeze swept along the ground, blowing the leaves before it. It struck the little fire and it seized one tiny flame and bore it up through the pile and about the legs of the imprisoned plebe.

The next instant the yearlings were thrown into the wildest imaginable confusion by a cry from one of them.

"Look out! Look out! His trousers are afire!"

CHAPTER XVIII

TO THE RESCUE

Things happened in a whirl of confusion after that. To the horrified cadets a thousand incidents seemed to crowd in at one moment.

In the first place there was the terrified captive, bound helplessly to the tree, his clothing on fire, himself shrieking at the top of his lungs. Then there were the yearlings themselves, all crying out with fright and alarm and rushing wildly in to drag the burning wood away. Finally there were other arrivals, whom, in the excitement, the yearlings scarcely noticed. There were two of them; one tore a knife from his pocket and cut the rope in a dozen places, the other flung off his jacket and wrapped it quickly about Indian's feet, extinguishing the flames. And then the two stood up and gazed at the rest—the frightened yearlings and their infuriated victim.

Infuriated? Yes, wildly infuriated! A change had come over Indian such as no one who knew him had ever seen before. The fire had not really hurt him; it had only ruined his clothing and scorched his legs enough to make him wild with rage. He had tugged at his bonds savagely; when he was cut free he had torn loose from the friendly stranger who had knelt to extinguish the fire, and made a savage rush at the badly scared cadets.

Indian's face was convulsed with passion. His arms were swinging wildly like a windmill's sails in a hurricane, while from his mouth rushed a volley of exclamations that would have frightened Captain Kidd and his pirate band.

It made no difference what he hit; the fat boy was too blind with rage to see. He must hit something! If a tree had lain in his path he would have started in on that. As luck would have it, however, the thing that was nearest to him was a yearling—Baby Edwards.

Baby could have been no more frightened if he had seen an

express train charging on him. He turned instantly and fled—where else would he flee but to his idol Bull? He hid behind that worthy; Bull put up his hands to defend himself; and the next instant Indian's flying arms reached the spot.

One savage blow on the nose sent Bull tumbling backward—over Baby. Indian, of course, could not stop and so did a somersault over the two.

There was a pretty mêlée after that. Baby was the first to emerge, covered with dirt and bruises. Indian got up second; he gazed about him, his rage still burning; he gave one snort, shook his head clear of the soil as an angry bull might; and then made another savage rush at Baby. Baby this time had no friend to hide behind; Harris was lying on the ground, face down, as a man might do to protect himself in a cyclone. And so Baby had no resource but flight; he took to his heels, the enraged plebe a few feet behind; and in half a minute more the pair were lost to sight and sound, far distant in the woods, Indian still pursuing.

It might be pleasant to follow them, for Indian in his rage was a sight to divert the gods. But there was plenty more happening at the scene of the fire, things that ought not be missed.

In the first place, who were the two new arrivals? It was evident that they were plebes—their faces were familiar to the cadets. But beyond that no one knew anything about them. They had freed their helpless classmate and saved him from serious injury, as has been told. They had done one thing more that has not been mentioned yet. One of them, the smaller, just after Indian had broken loose, had reached over and dealt the nearest yearling he could reach a ringing blow upon the cheek.

"Take that!" said he. "Bah Jove, you're a cur."

There was another mêlée after that.

Of course the setting fire to Indian had been a pure accident; but the two strangers did not know it. They saw in the whole thing a piece of diabolical cruelty. The yearling the wrath chanced to fall upon was Gus Murray—and his anger is left to the imagination. He sprang at the throat of the reckless plebe; and the rest of the crowd rushed to his aid, pausing just for an instant to size up the pair.

They did not seem "to be any great shucks." The taller was a big slouchy-looking chap in clothes that evidently bespoke the farmer, and possessing a drawl which quite as clearly indicated the situation of the farm—the prairies. Having cut Indian loose he was lounging lazily against the tree and regarding his more excitable companion with a good-natured grin.

The companion was even less awe-inspiring, for one had to look at him but an instant to see that he was one of the creatures whom all well-regulated boys despise—a dude. He wore a high collar, ridiculously high; he was slender and delicate looking, with the correct Fifth Avenue stoop to his shoulders and an attitude to his arms which showed that he had left his cane behind only on compulsion when he "struck the Point." And any doubts the yearlings may have had on this question were settled as the yearlings stared, for the object turned to the other and spoke.

"Aw say, Sleepy," said he, "come help me chastise these fellows, don't ye know."

As a fact there was but little choice in the matter, it was fight or die with the two, for at the same instant Gus Murray, wild with rage, had leaped forward and made a savage lunge at the dude.

What happened then Murray never quite knew. All he made out was that when he hit at the dude the dude suddenly ceased to be there. The yearling glanced around in surprise and discovered that his victim had slid coolly under his elbow and was standing over on the other side of the clearing—smiling.

The rest of the crowd, not in the least daunted by Murray's miss, rushed in to the attack; and a moment later a wild scrimmage was in progress, a scrimmage which defied the eye to comprehend and the pen to describe. The former never moved from the tree, but with his back flat against it and his great clumsy arms swinging like sledge hammers he stood and bid defiance to his share of the crowd.

The dude's tactics were just the opposite. He was light and slender, and should have been easy prey. That was what Bull Harris thought as he hastily arose from the spot where Indian had butted him and joined his eager comrades in the hunt. The hunt; a hunt it was, and no mistake. While the farmer stayed in one place, the dude seemed everywhere at once. Dodging, ducking, running, he seemed just to escape every blow that was aimed at him. He seemed even to turn somersaults, to the amazed yearlings, who had been looking for a dude and not an acrobat.

The dude did not dodge all the time, though; occasionally he would stop to cool the ardor of some especially excited cadet with a sudden punch where it wasn't looked for. Once also he stuck out his foot and allowed Bull Harris to get his legs caught in it, with a result that Bull's nose once more plowed the clearing.

The writer wishes it were his privilege to chronicle the fact that the two put the eight to flight; or that Indian, having put the Baby "to sleep," returned to perform yet greater prodigies of valor. It would be a pleasure to tell of all that, but on the other hand truth is a stubborn thing. Things do not always happen as they should in spite of the providence that is supposed to make them.

The farmer, after a five-minute gallant stand, was finally knocked down—from behind—and once down he was being fast pummeled into nothingness. The dude—his collar, much to his alarm, having wilted—was in the last stage of exhaustion. In fact, Bull had succeeded in landing a blow, the first of the afternoon for him. The dude was about to give up and perish, when assistance arrived. For these gallant heroes were not fated to conquer alone.

The first warning of the arrival of reinforcements was not the traditional trumpet call, nor the roll of a drum, nor even the tramp of soldiers, but a muttered "Wow!" This was followed by Texas himself, bursting through the bushes like a battering ram. Mark was at his side, and behind them came the Parson. Dewey, being rather crippled, brought up the rear.

The four lost no time in questions; they saw two plebes in distress, and they had met Indian on the warpath and learned the cause of the trouble. They knew it was their business to help and they "sailed right in" to do it.

Mark placed himself by the side of the panting "dude." Texas and the Parson made a V formation and speedily got the farmer to his feet and in fighting array once more. And after that the odds of the battle were more even.

It was a very brief battle, in fact. A mere skirmish after that. Mark's prowess was dreaded, and that of Texas but little less. After

Texas had chased two yearlings into the woods, and Mark had stretched out Bull—that was Bull's third time that afternoon—the ardor of the eight began to wane. It was not very long then before the attack stopped by mutual consent, and the combatants took to staring at each other instead.

The rage of Bull as he picked himself up and examined his damages must be imagined.

"You confounded plebes shall pay for this," he roared, "as sure as I'm alive."

"Now?" inquired Mark, smiling, rubbing his hands, and looking ready to resume hostilities.

"It's a case of blamed swelled head, that's what it is," growled the other, sullenly.

"Which," added the Parson's solemn voice, "might be somewhat more classically expressed by the sesquipedalian Hellenic vocable—ahem!—Megalacephalomania."

With which interesting bit of information—presented gratis—the Parson carefully laid his beloved "Dana" on the ground and sat down on it for safety.

"Why can't you plebes mind your business, anyhow?" snarled Gus Murray.

"That's what I say, too!" cried Bull.

"Curious coincidence!" laughed Dewey. "Reminds me of a story I once heard, b'gee—I guess it's most too long a story to tell through. Remind me of it, Mark, and I'll tell it to you some day. One of the most remarkable tales I ever heard, that! Told me by a fellow that used to run a sausage factory. It was right next door to a "Home for Homeless Cats," though, b'gee, I couldn't ever see how the cats were homeless if they had a home there. They didn't stay very long, though. That was the funniest part of it. They used to sit on the fence near the sausage factory, b'gee——"

Dewey could have prattled on that way till doomsday with unfailing good humor. It made the yearlings mad and that was all he cared about. But by this time Bull had perceived that he was being guyed, and he turned away with an angry exclamation.

"You fellows may stay if you choose;" he said, "I'm going back to camp. And those plebes shall pay for this!"

"Cash on demand!" laughed Mark, as the discomfited crowd turned and slunk off.

CHAPTER XIX

THE ALLIANCE IS COMPLETED

Having been thus easily rid of their unpleasant enemies, the plebes set out in high feather for home.

"I must get back in time to dress for dinner, don't ye know," said the dude.

"I'm 'bliged to yew fellows," put in the farmer, getting up from his seat with a lazy groan. "My name's Methusalem Zebediah Chilvers, and I'll shake hands all raound."

"And mine's Chauncey Van Rensallear Mount-Bonsall, don't ye know," said the other, putting on his immaculate white gloves. "Bah Jove! I've lost a cuff button, quarreling with those deuced yearlings!"

Chauncey's cuff button was found at last—he vowed he wouldn't go to dinner without it—and then the party started in earnest, the two strangers giving a graphic and characteristic account of the scrimmage we have just witnessed.

Mark in the meantime was doing some thinking, wondering if here were not two more eligible members of the "alliance." While he was debating this question the "dude" approached him privately and began thus:

"I want to say something to you," he said. "Dye know, I can't see why we plebes suffer so, bah Jove! I was thinking aw, don't ye know, if some of us would band together we could—aw—chastise the deuced cadets and——"

Master Chauncey Van Rensallear Mount-Bonsall got no further, for Mark came out then and told the secret. In a few moments the alliance had added Number Six and Number Seven.

"And now, b'gee, I say let's organize, b'gee!" cried Dewey.

The sound of a drum from barracks put a stop to further business then, but before supper there was a spare half hour, and during that time the seven conspirators met in Mark's room to "organize." Indian was there, too, now calm and meek again.

"In the first place," said Mark, "we want to elect a leader."

"Wow!" cried Texas, "what fo'? Ain't you leader?"

"I say, Mark, b'gee!" cried Dewey.

"Mark," said the Parson, solemnly.

"Mark," murmured Indian from the corner, and "Mark" chimed in the two newcomers.

"It seems to be unanimous," said Mark, "so I guess I'll have to let it go. But I'm sure I can't see why you think of me. What shall we call ourselves?"

That brought a lengthy discussion, which space does not permit of being given. The Loyal Legion, the Sons of the Revolution, the Independents, the Cincinnati—suggested by the classic Parson—and also the Trojan Heroes—from the same source—all these were suggested and rejected. Then somebody moved the Seven Rebels, which was outvoted as not expressive enough, but which led to another one that took the whole crowd with a rush. It came from an unexpected source—the unobtrusive Indian in the corner.

"Let's name it 'The Seven Devils'!" said he.

And the Seven Devils they were from that day until the time when the class graduated from the Point.

"Three cheers for the Seven Devils!" cried Dewey, "b'gee!"

"Now," said the Parson, rising with a solemn look, "let us swear eternal fealty by all that man holds holy. Let us swear by the Stygian Shades and the realms of Charon, whence all true devils come. Yea, by Zeus!"

"And we'll stand by one another to the death, b'gee," cried Dewey. "Remember, we're organized for no purpose on earth but to do those yearlings, and we'll lick 'em, b'gee, if they dare to look at us."

"Show 'em no mercy, don't ye know," said "Chauncey."

"And let's have a motto," cried Indian, becoming infected with the excitement. "'Down with the yearlings.'"

"I suggest 'We die but we never surrender,' b'gee."

"'Veni, vidi, vici,'" remarked the Parson, "or else 'Dulce et decorum est pro patria mori,' in the immortal words of Horace, poet of the Sabine farm."

"A motto should be brief," laughed Mark. "I can beat you all. I'll give you a motto in three letters of the alphabet."

"Three letters!" echoed the crowd. "Three letters! What is it?"

"It expresses all our objects in forming," said Mark, "and we'll have lots of fun if we obey it. My motto is 'B. B. J.'"

"Bully, b'gee!" cried Dewey, and the rest echoed his approval with a rush.

That was, all except the unobtrusive Indian in the corner.

"I—I don't quite," he stammered, "quite see it. Why is——"

"Ahem!" Mark straightened himself up and put on his best professional air in imitation of the Parson. "Ahem! If you had lived in Boston, and devoted yourself to the cultivation of the intellectualities—yea, by Zeus!—instead of learning to lose your temper and chase yearlings like a wild Texan—— However, I'll explain it."

"Please do!" cried Indian, innocently. "I'll never chase the yearlings again."

"That's good! B. J. stands for 'before June,' and is West Point slang for 'fresh.'"

"I knew what B. J. means," put in Indian.

"What! Then why didn't you say so and save me the trouble? The other B. is the present imperative of the verb to be; he was, being, been, is, am, ain't. And the only way I can explain what B. B. J. means is to say that it means be B. J., be B. J. with a vengeance, and when you get tired of being B. J., B. B. J. some more. Do you see?"

"Er, yes," said Indian.

"And now," laughed Mark, "since we're through, three cheers for the Seven Devils!"

And that is the story of the forming of West Point's first and only secret society, a society which was destined to introduce some very, very exciting incidents into West Point's dignified history, the Seven Devils, B. B. J.

CHAPTER XX

INDIGNATION OF THE YEARLINGS

"By George, he's the freshest plebe that ever struck this place!"

The speaker was Bull Harris, and he was sitting on the steps of the library building along with half a dozen classmates, excitedly and angrily discussing the fight.

"Now I tell you Mark Mallory's got to be put out of this place in a week," continued the first speaker. "And I don't care how it's done, either, fair or foul."

"That's just what I say, too!" chimed in Baby Edwards. "He's got to be put out in a week!"

Bull Harris smiled benignly upon his toadying echo, while the rest of the gang nodded approvingly.

"I'm sure everybody agrees that he's got to be taken down," put in somebody else. "The only trouble is I don't see how on earth it is to be done."

"That's the worst of it!" snarled Bull. "That fellow Mallory seems to get the best of us everything we try; confound him!"

"I'm sure such a thing has never been known at West Point," said another. "Just think of it! Why, it's the talk of the post, and everybody's laughing at us, and the plebes are getting bolder every minute. One of them actually dared to turn up his nose at me to-day. Think of it—at me—a yearling, and he a vile beast!"

"It's perfectly awful," groaned Bull. "Perfectly awful! Imagine a crowd of yearlings allowing themselves to be stopped while hazing a plebe—stopped, mind you, by half as many plebes—and then to make it a thousand times worse to have the fellow they were hazing taken away!"

"And the yearlings all chased back to camp by a half-crazy Texan," chimed in another, who hadn't been there and so could afford to mention unpleasant details.

"Yet what can we do?" cried Baby. "We can't offer to fight him. He's as good as licked Billy Williams, and Bill's the best man we could put up. That Mallory's a regular terror."

"Mark Mallory's got to be taken down."

This suggestion was good, only rather indefinite, which indefiniteness was remarked by one of the crowd, Merry Vance, the cadet who had interposed the same objection before. Merry was a tall, slender youth, with a whitish hue that suggested dissipation, and a fine, scornful curve to his lips that suggested meanness no less clearly.

"It's all very well to say we've got to do him," said he, "but that don't say how. As I said, we can't find a man in our class to whip him fair. And we can't tackle him in a crowd because in the first place he seems to have his own gang, and in the second place none of us dares to touch him. I know I don't, for one."

"Pooh!" laughed Bull, scornfully. "I'm not afraid of him."

"Me either!" chimed in the little Baby, doubling up his fists.

"All right," said the other. "Only I noticed you both kept good and quiet when he stepped up to loosen Indian."

There was an awkward silence for a few minutes after that; Bull Harris could think of nothing to say, for he knew the charge was true; and as for Baby Edwards, he never said anything until after his big friend had set him an example.

"We can't get him into any trouble with the authorities, either," continued Vance at last. "In fact, I don't know what we are to do."

"He's simply turned West Point's customs topsy-turvy," groaned another. "Why, when we were plebes nobody ever dared to think of defying a yearling. And this Mallory and his gang are running the place. No one dares to haze a plebe any more."

"Talking about that," said Gus Murray, another yearling who had just strolled up. "Talking about that, just see what happened to me not five minutes ago. Met one of the confounded beasts—that fellow, by the way, we did up, though it don't seem to have done him the least bit of good—just as B. J. as ever. You know who I mean, the rather handsome chap they call Dewey. He went to pass the color guard up at camp just now and he didn't raise his hat. The sentry called him down for it, and then as he went off I said to him: 'You ought to know better than that, plebe.' 'Thank you,' says he, and when I told him he should say 'sir' to a higher cadet, what on earth do you suppose he had the impudence to say?"

"What?" inquired the crowd, eagerly.

"Said he wouldn't do it because I hadn't said 'sir' to him!"

"What!"

"Yes, indeed! Did you ever hear of such impudence? Why, I'll leave the academy to-morrow if that kind of thing keeps up."

And with that dire threat Gus Murray seated himself on the steps and relapsed into a glum silence.

"I heard you sat down on that Mallory last Saturday," observed some one at last.

"That's what I did!" responded Murray, brightening up at the mention of a less discouraging incident. "Mary Adams introduced me to him and I cut him dead. Gee, but he was mad!"

"Wonder, if he'll try to make you apologize," said Bull.

"It would be just like him," put in Merry.

The other looked as if he didn't relish the possibility one bit; he turned the conversation quickly.

"Wait till he tries it," said he. "In the meantime I'm more interested in the great question, what are we going to do to take him down?"

"Can't think of a thing," said Vance, flatly. "Not a thing!"

"By George!" cried Bull. "I'm going to think of something if I die for it."

"I'll shake with you on that," put in Murray. "We won't rest till we get a plan."

"Let me in too," said Vance.

"And me too!" cried Baby.

And so it happened that when the informal assembly dissolved for supper it dissolved with but one idea in the mind of every cadet in the party—that Mark Mallory must be taken down!

A plan came at last, one which was enough to do for any one; and when it came it came from a most unexpected source, none other than the Baby, who never before in the memory of Bull had dared to say anything original. The baby's sweet little brain, evolving the interesting problem, struck an idea which, so to speak, brought down the house.

"I'll tell you what!" he cried. "I've a scheme!"

"What is it?" inquired Bull, incredulously.

"Let's soak him on demerits!"

And with a look of delight Bull turned and stared at Murray.

"By the lord!" he cried, "that's it. We'll soak him on demerits!"

Then the precious trio locked arms and did a war on the campus.

"Just the thing!" gasped Bull, breathlessly. "Murray's a corporal and he can do it! Whoop!"

"Yes!" cried the Baby. "And he was put over plebes to-day. Will you do it, Murray?"

And Murray lost no time in vowing that he would; Bull Harris felt then that at last he was on the road to victory.

It is necessary to explain the system of discipline which prevails at West Point. A cadet is allowed to receive only one hundred "demerits" during the first six months of his stay. These demerits are assigned according to a regular and inflexible schedule; thus for being late at roll call, a minor offense, a cadet receives two demerits, while a serious offense, such as disobedience of orders or sitting down on post while on sentry duty, brings ten units of trouble in its wake. These demerits are not given by the instructor or the cadet who notices the offense; but he enters the charge in a book which is forwarded to headquarters. The report is read out after parade that same day and posted in a certain place the next day; and four days later the superintendent assigns the demerits in all cases where "explanations" have not been received.

The following is an example of an explanation:

"West Point, N. Y., —— ——, 18—. Report—Bedding not properly folded at police inspection.

"Explanation—Some one disarranged my bedding after I had piled it. I was at the sink at the time of inspection, and I readjusted the bedding upon my return.

"Respectfully submitted,

"—— ——,

"Cadet ——, Co. ——, —— Class.

"To the Commandant of Cadets."

Cadets usually hand in explanations, though the explanations are not always deemed satisfactory.

Reports are made by the army officers, and also by cadets themselves, file closers, section marchers and others. It was in this last fact that Bull Harris and his friend Murray saw their chance.

It very seldom happens that a cadet reports another except where the report is deserved; a man who does otherwise soon gets into trouble. But Bull and his gang saw no obstacle in that; most of them were always head over heels in demerits themselves, including Murray—though he was a "cadet-corporal." Being thus, and in consequent danger of expulsion, they were reckless of possible trouble. And besides, Bull had sworn to haze that plebe, and he meant to do it.

The plan in brief was simply this: Mark Mallory must be demerited right and left, everywhere and upon every possible pretext, just or unjust—and that was all. The thing has been done before; there is talk of doing it whenever a colored lad is admitted to the Point. And Murray was the man to do it, too, because he had just been transferred and put "on duty over plebes." It was only necessary to give one hundred demerits. One hundred demerits is a ticket of leave without further parley or possibility of return.

CHAPTER XXI

A MILD ATTEMPT AT HAZING

If Cadet Corporal Murray had any doubts about the necessity for putting this very dirty scheme into practice, or if his not over squeamish conscience was the least bit troubled by the prospect, something happened that same evening which effectually squelched such ideas. It was after supper, during half an hour of so-called "rest," which is allowed to the over-drilled plebe. Mr. Murray, in whose manly breast still burned a fire of rage at the insult which "B. J." Dewey had offered him, resolved in his secret heart that that same insult must and should be avenged. That evening he thought an especially favorable time, for Dewey was still an "invalid," as a result of his last B. J. effort.

With this purpose in view, Cadet Murray stole away from his companions and set out for barracks, around which the luckless plebes were clustered. Arriving there, he hunted; he spent quite a while in hunting, for the object of his search was nowhere to be seen. He caught sight of Mark and his "gang," but Dewey was not among them. When he did find him at last it was a good way from that place—way up on Flirtation Walk; and then Cadet Murray got down to business at once.

"Look a here, B. J. beast!" he called.

The object of this peremptory challenge turned, as also did his companion, the terrified Indian—once more about to be hazed. The two stared at the yearling; a lady and gentleman passing glanced at him also, probably wondering what was in store for the luckless plebes; and then they passed on, leaving the place lonely, and deserted, just the spot for the proposed work. So thought the yearling, as he rubbed his hands gleefully and spoke again.

"Beast!" said he, "I want to tell you that you were very impudent to me to-day!"

"Strange coincidence!" cried Dewey, with one of his merry laughs. "Reminds me of a story I once heard, b'gee. Two old farmers got stuck in a snowdrift—five feet deep, and getting deeper. Says one of 'em, b'gee, 'It's c-c-c-cold!' 'B'gee!' cried the other. 'B'gee, naow ain't that pecooliar! Jes' exactly what I was goin' to say myself, b'gee!'"

Cadet Murray listened to this blithe recital with a frowning brow.

"You think that's funny, don't you!" he sneered.

"No, b'gee!" laughed Dewey, "because I didn't write it. 'Nother fellow told me that—the queerest chap I think I ever knew, he was. Had a mother-in-law that used to——"

"Shut up!" cried Murray, in anger, seeing that he was being "guyed."

"B'gee!" cried Dewey, "that's just what she didn't!"

There was an ominous silence after that, during which the yearling glared angrily, and Indian muttered "Bless my soul!"

"It's quite evident," began the former, at last, "that you are inclined to be fresh."

"Ink-lined to be fresh," added Dewey, "as the stamped egg remarked when it was dated three days after it was laid. That's another far-fetched joke, though. Still I've heard some more far-fetched than that—one a friend of mine read on an Egyptian pyramid and brought home to tell for new. Queer fellow that friend of mine was, too. He didn't have a mother-in-law, this one, but he slept in a folding bed, and, b'gee, that bed used to shut up oftener than the mother-in-law didn't. Handsome bed, too—an inlaid bed— and it shut up whenever it was laid in, b'gee."

Dewey could have prattled on at this merry rate for an hour, for he knew more jokes—good ones—and could make up more bad ones on the spur of the moment than half a dozen ordinary mortals. But he was brought to a sudden halt just then, and muttered a suppressed "B'gee!" For the yearling, wild with anger, leaped forward and aimed a savage blow at his head.

The plebe ducked; he was quick and agile in body as he was in mind. And then as the big cadet aimed another blow, he put up his one well arm—the other was in a sling—and defended himself to the best of his ability, at the same time calling Indian to his aid.

But before there was time for another move something else

happened. Dewey was debating whether discretion were not really the whole of valor, and whether it were not better to "run away and live to fight—or run away—some other day;" and Indian was actually doubling up his fat little fists about to strike the first blow in his fat little life; when suddenly came a shout behind them, and a moment later a strong hand seized the advancing yearling by the back of his collar and flung him head first to the ground.

Cadet Murray sprang to his feet again and turned purple with rage and soiled with dirt, to confront the stalwart form of Mark, and Mark rubbing his hands together and smiling cheerfully.

"Will you have any more?" he inquired, politely. "Step right up if you will—and by the way, stop that swearing."

"A very timely arrival," remarked Dewey, smoothing his jacket. "Very timely, b'gee! Reminds me——"

"Bless my soul!" cried Indian.

"Going, are you?" put in Mark, as the discomfited Murray started to slink away. "Well, good-evening. I've had my satisfaction for being called a coward by you."

"You shall pay for this," the furious cadet muttered. "Pay for it as sure as I'm alive!"

His threat was taken lightly by the plebes; they had little idea of what he meant when he spoke. And they were chatting merrily about the adventure as they turned and made their way back to barracks.

"It only goes to show," was Mark's verdict, "that an alliance is a first-rate idea. I saw that fellow prowling around barracks and I knew right away what he was up to. We've one more enemy, that's all."

That was not all, by a good sight. The angry yearling hurried back to camp, nursing his feelings as he went; there he poured out the vials of his wrath into the ears of his two sympathetic companions, Bull and the Baby. And the three of them spent the rest of that evening, up to tattoo, discussing their revenge, thinking up a thousand pretexts upon which Cadet Mallory might be "skinned." There was a bombshell scheduled to fall into the midst of the "alliance" the next day.

CHAPTER XXII

THE BOMBSHELL FALLS

Nothing happened that evening; Mark and his friends passed their time in serene unconsciousness of any danger, merrily discussing the latest hazing effort of the enemy. Bull Harris and his crowd did not put in appearance, or try to put their plot into execution, for the simple reason that there was no chance. The first "whack," so to speak, was scheduled for the A. M. inspection the next day. The only inspection at night is made by a "tac"—a practical officer—who goes the rounds with a dark lantern after taps to make sure that no plebes have been run away with.

Reveille and roll call the next morning passed without incident, except that Cadet Mallory was reported "late" at the latter function; the charge being true, no suspicions were awakened. After that came the march to mess hall, the plebe company, which was by this time able to march presentably though rather stiffly, falling in behind the rest of the corps. During that march "File Closer" Vance had occasion to rebuke Cadet Mallory for loud talking in ranks. It hadn't been loud, at least not very loud, but Mark swallowed it and said nothing.

Breakfast passed without incident, and the plebes were marched back to barracks, there breaking ranks, and scattering to quarters to "spruce up" for inspection. Mark and Texas, who shared the same room, lost no time in getting to work at the sweeping and dusting and arranging.

It seems scarcely necessary to say that there are no chambermaids at West Point. Cadets do their own room cleaning, "policing," as it is called, and they do it well, too. A simpler, barer place than a room in barracks it would be hard to imagine. Bare white walls—no pictures allowed—and no wall paper—a black fireplace, a plain table, an iron bedstead, a washstand, two chairs, and a window is about the entire inventory. And every article in that room must be found placed with mathematical precision in just such a spot and no other. There is a "bluebook"—learned by heart—to tell where; and there are penalties for every infringement. Demerits are the easiest things in the world to get; enough might be given at one inspection to expel.

The signal, dreaded like poison by all plebes, that the time for inspection has come, is a heavy step in the hall and a single tap upon the door. It came that morning while the two victims-to-be were still hard at work. In accordance with orders each sprang up, stood at attention—heels together, head up, eyes to the front, chest out, etc.—and silently awaited developments.

Mark gasped for breath when he saw who it was that entered; Cadet Corporal Jasper had been transferred and the man who was to do the work this time was none other than Murray, next to Bull Harris, Mark's greatest enemy on earth.

Cadet Murray looked handsome in his spotless uniform of gray and white, with his chevrons of gold; he strode in with a stern and haughty look which speedily changed to one of displeasure as he gazed about him at the room. He took a rapid mental count of the possible charges he could make; and then glanced up at the name which is posted on the wall, telling who is "room orderly" for the week—and so responsible for the faults. It was Mallory, and the yearling could scarcely hide a smile of satisfaction.

"You plebes have had nearly two weeks now," he began, frowning with well-feigned displeasure, "in which to learn to arrange your rooms. The disorder which I see shows not only carelessness but actual insubordination. And I propose to make an example of you two for once and for all."

The two victims were expected to say nothing; and they said it. But Mark did a pile of thinking and his heart sank as he realized what his enemy might do if he chose. It is possible to find a thousand faults in the most perfect work if one only hunts long enough and is willing to split hairs.

Cadet Corporal Murray took out a notebook and pencil with obvious meaning.

"In the first place," said he, "where should that broom be? Behind the door, should it not? Why is it not? I find that your bedding is piled carelessly, very carelessly. The blanket is not evenly folded; moreover, the bluebook states particularly that the blanket is to be placed at the bottom of the pile. You may see that it is not so. Why, Mr. Mallory, I do not think it has ever happened to me to find a room so utterly disorderly, or a cadet so negligent! Look at that bluebook; it belongs upon the mantelpiece, and I see it on the bed——"

"I was reading it," put in Mark, choking down his anger by a violent effort.

And as he spoke the corporal's face grew sterner yet.

"In the first place, sir," said he, "you have no business to be reading while awaiting inspection, and you know it—though I must say a more frequent study of that book would save you much trouble. In the second place, you are not expected to answer under such circumstances; the proper thing for you to do is to hand in the explanation to the authorities, and you know that, too. I am sent here to notice and report delinquencies and not to argue about them with you. I regret now that I shall be obliged to mention the fact that you remonstrated with an officer during inspection, a most serious charge indeed."

And Cadet Corporal Murray made another note in his book, chuckling inwardly as he did it.

"What next?" thought the two plebes.

There was lots more. The yearling next stepped over to the mantelpiece and ran his finger, with its spotless white glove, along the inner edge. Texas had rubbed that mantel fiercely; yet, to get it so clean as not to soil the glove was almost impossible, and so the corporal first held up the finger to show the mark of dirt and then— wrote down "dust on mantel."

There is no need to tell the rest in detail, but simply to say that while Mark and his roommate gazed on in blank despair, their jubilant enemy made out a list of at least a dozen charges, which he knew would aggregate to at least half of the demerit maximum, and for every one of which there was some slight basis of justification. The yearling was shrewd enough to suspect this fact would prevent their being excused, for he did not think that Mark would sign his name to a lie in his explanation.

The disastrous visit was closed with a note—"floor unswept"—

because three scraps of paper were observed peering out from under the table; and then without another word the cadet turned on his heel and marched out of the room. And Mark and Texas stood and stared at each other in utter and abject consternation.

It was a minute at least before either of them spoke; they were both too dumfounded. The bombshell had struck, and had brought ruin in its path. Mark knew now what was the power of his enemies; knew that he was gone. For with such a weapon as the one the cowardly Murray had struck his dismissal was the matter of a week or less. Already he was more than halfway to expulsion; already the prize for which he had fought so long and so hard was slipping from his grasp. And all on account of a cowardly crowd he had made his enemies because he had been strong and manly enough to do what he knew was right.

It was a cruel fact and Mark felt pretty bitter toward West Point just then. As for Texas, his faithful friend and roommate, Texas said not one word; but he went to the chimney, up which he had hidden his sixteen revolvers for safety, calmly selected two of the biggest, and having examined the cartridges, tucked them safely away in his rear pockets. Then he sat down on the bed and gave vent to a subdued "Durnation!"

About this same time Cadet Corporal Murray, having handed in his reports at headquarters, was racing joyfully back to camp, there to join his friend, Bull Harris, with a shout of victory.

"Rejoice! Rejoice!" he cried, slapping his chum on the back. "We've got him! I soaked him for fifty at least!"

CHAPTER XXIII

IN THE SHADOW OF DISMISSAL

The rest of that day passed without incident. Mark managed after a good deal of trouble to postpone Texas' hunting trip; and the two struggled on through the day's drills disconsolately, waiting to see what would happen next.

Evening came, and the plebes being lined up in barracks area the roll was called, the "orders" read, and then the reports of the day. The cadet who did the reading rattled down the list in his usual hurried, breathless style. But when he came to M he paused suddenly; he gazed at the list incredulously, then cleared his throat, took a long foreboding breath and began:

"Mallory—Late at roll call.

"Same—Laughing loud in ranks.

"Same—Bedding improperly arranged at A. M. inspection.

"Same—Broom out of place at A. M. inspection.

"Same—Remonstrating with superior officer at A. M. inspection."

And so the cadet officer went on, the whole plebe class listening with open-eyed amazement while one charge after another was rattled off, and gazing out of the corners of their eyes at the object of the attack, who stood and listened with a look of calm indifference upon his face.

The list was finished at last, when the listeners had about concluded that it was eternal; the rest of the reports were quickly disposed of, and then: "Break ranks, march!" and the line melted into groups of excited and eagerly talking cadets, discussing but one subject—the ruin of Mallory.

Of course it was known to every one that this was simply one more effort of the yearlings to subdue him; and loud were the threats and expressions of disapproval. Mark's bravery in making a fight for his honor had won him the admiration of his class, and the class felt that with his downfall came a return of the old state of affairs and the complete subjection of the "beasts" once more.

There were jealous ones who rejoiced secretly, and there were timid ones who declared that they had always said that Mallory was too B. J. to last. But in the main there was nothing but genuine anger at the upper classmen's "rank injustice," and wild talk of appealing to the superintendent to bring it to a stop.

The utter consternation of the seven allies is left to the reader's imagination. After the first shock of horror had passed the crowd had sat down and made a calculation; they found fifty-five demerits due that day, which, together with ten previously given, left thirty-five to go, and then—why it made them sick to think of what would happen!

Having striven to realize this for half an hour, they got together and swore a solemn oath, first, that if Mark were dismissed, a joint statement of the reasons thereof, incidentally mentioning each and every act of hazing done by the yearlings, naming principals, witnesses, time and place, should be forwarded to the superintendent, signed by the six; and second, that every yearling who gave a demerit should be "licked until he couldn't stand up."

Texas also swore incidentally that he'd resign if Mark were "fired," and take him down to Texas to make a cowboy of him. And after that there was nothing to do but wait and pray—and clean up for next day's inspection, a task at which the whole seven labored up to the very last minute before tattoo.

It was the afternoon of the following day; the rays of a scorching July sun beat down upon the post, and West Point seemed asleep. Up by Camp McPherson the cadets were lounging about in idleness, and it was only down at barracks that there was anything moving at all. Inside the area the hot and shimmering pavement echoed to the tread of the plebe company at drill; outside the street was deserted except for one solitary figure with whom our story has to do. The figure was a cadet officer in uniform, Captain Fischer, of the first class, resplendent in his chevrons and sash.

He was marching down the street with the firm, quick step that is second nature to a West Pointer; he passed the barracks without looking in and went on down to the hospital building; and there he turned and started to enter. The door opened just as he reached it, however, and another cadet came out. The officer sprang forward instantly and grasped him by the hand.

"Williams!" he cried. "Just the fellow I was coming to see. And what a beautiful object you are!"

Williams smiled a melancholy smile; he was beautiful and he knew it. His face was covered in spots with Greek crosses of court-plaster, and elsewhere by startling red lumps. And he walked with a shy, retiring gait that told of sundry other damages. Such were the remains of handsome "Billy," all-round athlete and favorite of his class, defeated hero.

Williams had waited scarcely long enough for this thought to flash over the young officer before he spoke again, this time with some anxiety.

"Tell me! Tell me about Mallory! I hear they're skinning him on demerits."

"Yes, they are," returned Fischer, "and they've soaked him twenty more this morning!"

"Twenty more! Then how many has he?"

"Eighty-five."

"What!" cried Williams. "You don't mean it! Why, he'll be out in a week. Say, Fischer, that's outrageous!"

"Perfectly outrageous!" vowed the officer.

And Williams brought his hand down on his knee with a bang.

"By George!" he cried, "I'm going around to see him about it!"

With which words he sprang down the stairs and, leaving the cadet officer to gaze at him in surprise, hurried up the street to barracks.

Squad drill was just that moment over; without wasting any time about it, Williams hurried into the building and made his way to Mallory's room. He found the plebe, and got right to work to say what he had to say.

"Mr. Mallory," he began, "I've come up in the first place to shake hands with you, and to say there's no hard feeling."

"Thank you," said Mark, and his heart went with the grip of his hand.

"You made a good fight, splendid!" continued the yearling. "And some day I'll be proud to be your friend."

"I'm afraid," returned Mark, with a sad smile, "that I'll not be here that long."

"That's the second thing I've come to see you about," vowed Williams. "Mr. Mallory, I want you to understand that the decent men of this class don't approve of the work that Mur—er, I suppose you know who's back of it. And I tell you right now that I'm going to stop it if it's the last act I ever do on this earth!"

"I'm afraid it won't do much good," responded the other, shaking his head. "I could never pass six months without getting fifteen demerits."

"It's a shame!" cried the other. "And you have worked for your appointment, too."

"I have worked," exclaimed Mark, something choking his voice that sounded suspiciously near a sob, "worked for it as I have never worked for anything in my life. It has been the darling ambition of my heart to come here. And I came—and now—and now——"

He stopped, for he could think of no more to say. Williams stood and regarded him in silence for some moments, and then he took him by the hand again.

"Mr. Mallory," said he, "just as sure as I'm alive this thing shall stop! Keep up heart now, and we'll make a fight for it! While there's life there's hope, they say—and, by Heaven, you shan't be expelled!"

The following evening, when the reports were read, Mark's list of demerits had reached a total of ninety-five.

The excitement among plebes and cadets alike was intense, and it was known far and wide that Mark Mallory, the "B. J." plebe, stood at last "in the shadow of dismissal."

CHAPTER XXIV

A LETTER

"My Dear Fischer: I promised to drop you a line just to let you know how I'm getting along, though it does take a tremendous pile of energy to write a letter on a hot afternoon like this. I'm sure I shall go to sleep in the middle of it, and naturally, too, for even writing to you is enough to bore anybody. I can almost imagine you leaning over to whack at me in return for that compliment.

"Well, I am home on furlough; and I don't know whether I wish I were back or not, for I fear that you will have cut me out on all the girls, especially since you are a high and mighty first captain this year. Speaking of girls, you just ought to be here. The girls at West Point are blasé on cadets, for they see so many; but here a West Point officer is cock of the walk, and I have to fight a jealous rival once a week."

Cadet Captain Fischer dropped the letter at this stage of it and lay back and laughed.

"Wicks Merritt's evidently forgotten I was on furlough once myself," he said. "He's telling me all about how it goes."

"What's he got to say?" inquired Williams, the speaker's tentmate, looking up from the gun he was cleaning.

"Oh, nothing much; only a lot of nonsense—jollying as usual. Wicks always is."

And then Fischer picked up the letter again, and went on.

The two were seated near the door of a tent in "Company A Street," at Camp McPherson. Fischer was lying in front of the tent "door," which was open to admit the morning breeze that swept across the parade ground. His friend sat over in an opposite corner and rubbed away.

There was silence of some minutes, broken only by the sound

of the polishing and the rustling of Fischer's paper. And then the latter spoke again.

"Oh, say!" said he. "Here's something that'll interest you, Billy. Something about your friend Mallory."

"Fire away," said Williams.

"'By the way, when you answer this let me know something about my pet and protégé, future football captain of the West Point eleven. The last time I heard from where you are, Mark Mallory was raising Cain. I heard that he was a B. J. plebe for fair; that he'd set to work to make war on the yearlings, and had put them to rout in style; also, incidentally, that he was scheduled to fight Billy Williams, the yearling's pet athlete. Tell Billy I hope the plebe does him; tell him I say that if Mallory once whacks him on the head with that right arm of his he'll see more stars from the lick than the Lick telescope can show— —'"

"Billy" broke in just then with a dismal groan.

"I don't know whether that's because of the pun," laughed Fischer, "or because of your recollection of the blow. However, I'll proceed.

"'Now, I don't care how much you fellows haze my Mallory; he's tough and he can stand it. He'll probably give you tit for tat every time, anyhow. But I do want to say this—watch out that nobody tries any foul play on him, skins him on demerits or reports him unfairly. Do me a favor and keep your eye out for that. Watch particularly Bull Harris, who is, I think, the meanest sneak in the yearling class, and also his chum, Gus Murray.

"'I know it for a fact that Mallory caught Bull in a very dirty act about a month ago and knocked spots out of him for it. I can't tell you what the act was; but Bull has sworn vengeance and he'll probably try to get it, so watch for me. If you let Mallory get into trouble, mind what I say, I'll never forgive you as long as you live. I'll cut you out with Bessie Smith, who, they say, is your fair one at present. Mallory is a treasure, and when you know him as well as I you'll think so, too.'"

Cadet Captain Fischer dropped the letter, sat up, and stared at Williams; and Williams stared back. There was disgust on the faces of both.

"By George!" cried the latter at last, striking his gunstock in the ground. "By George! we've let 'em do it already!"

And after that there was a silence of several unpleasant minutes, during which each was diligently thinking over the situation.

"He's a fine fellow, anyway," continued Williams. "And we were a pack of fools to let that Bull Harris gang soak him as we did. They've gone to work and given him ninety-five demerits in a week on trumped-up charges. And it's perfectly outrageous, that's what it is! The plebe's confoundedly fresh, of course, but he's a gentleman for all that, and he don't deserve one-quarter of the demerits he's gotten. The decent fellows in the class ought to be ashamed of themselves."

"That's what I say! He only has to get five demerits more and then he's fired for good."

"Which means," put in the officer, "that's he's sure to be fired by next week."

"Exactly! And then what will Wicks say? I went over to barracks to see Mallory about it yesterday; he's nearly heart-broken, for he's worked like a horse to get here, and now he's ruined—practically expelled. Yet, what can we do?"

"Can't he hand in explanations and get the demerits excused?" suggested Fischer.

"No, because most of the charges had just enough basis of truth in them to make them justifiable. I tell you I was mad when he told me about it; I vowed I'd do something to stop it. Yet what on earth can I do? I can't think of a thing except to lick that fellow Bull Harris and his crowd. But what possible good will that do Mallory?"

"Mallory will probably do that himself," remarked Fischer,

smiling for a moment; his face became serious again as he continued. "I begin to agree with you, Billy, about that thing. I've heard several tales about how Mallory outwitted Bull in his hazing adventures, and the plebe's probably made him mad. It's a dirty revenge Bull has taken, and I think if it's only for Wicks' sake I'll put a stop to it."

"You!" echoed Williams. "Pray, how?"

"What am I a first captain for?" laughed Fischer. "Just you watch me and see what I do! I can't take off the ninety-five, but I can see that he don't get the other five, by Jingo! And I will do it for you, too!"

And with that, the cadet arose and strode out of the tent, leaving his friend to labor at the gun in glum and disconsolate silence.

At the same time that Williams and Fischer were discussing the case of this particularly refractory plebe, there were other cadets doing likewise, but with far different sentiments and views. The cadets were Bull Harris and his cronies.

They were sitting—half a dozen of them—beneath the shade trees of Trophy Point at the northern end of the parade ground; they were waiting for dinner, and the afternoon, which, being Saturday, was a holiday and for which they had planned some particular delicious hazing adventure.

Foremost among them was Bull Harris himself, seated upon one of the cannon. Beside him was Baby Edwards. Gus Murray sat on Bull's other side and made up a precious trio.

Murray was laughing heartily at something just then, and the rest of the crowd seemed to appreciate the joke immensely.

"Ho! ho!" said he. "Just think of it! After I had soaked the confounded plebe for fifty and more, ho! ho! they got suspicious up at headquarters and transferred me, and ho! ho! put M-m-merry Vance on instead, and he, ho! ho! soaked him all the harder!"

And Gus Murray slapped his knee and roared at this truly humorous state of affairs.

"Yes," chimed in Merry Vance. "Yes, I thought when Gus told me he'd been transferred again that we'd lost our chance to skin Mallory for fair. And the very next night up gets the adjutant and reads off the orders putting me on duty over the plebes. Oh, gee! Did you ever hear the like?"

"Never," commented Bull, grinning appreciatively.

"Never," chimed in Baby's little voice. "Positively never!"

"Tell us about it," suggested another. "What did you do?"

"Oh, nothing much," replied Vance. "I went up there at the A. M. inspection, and I just made up my mind to give him twenty demerits, and I did it, that's all. They had spruced up out of sight; but it didn't take me very long to find something wrong, I tell you."

"I guess not!" agreed Baby.

"I gave him the twenty, as you saw; and say, you ought to have seen how sick he looked! Ho! ho!"

And then the crowd indulged in another fit of violent hilarity.

"I guess," said Bull, when this had finally passed, "that we can about count Mallory as out for good. He's only got five more demerits to run before dismissal, and he'll be sure to get those in time, even if we don't give 'em to him—which, by the way, I mean to do anyhow. But we'll just parcel 'em one at a time just enough to keep him worried, hey?"

"That's it exactly!" commented the Baby.

"He deserves it every bit!" growled Bull. "He's the B. J.est 'beast' that ever struck West Point. Why, we could never have a moment's peace with that fellow around. We couldn't haze anybody. He stopped us half a dozen times."

The sentiment was the sentiment of the whole gang; and they felt that they had cause to be happy indeed. Their worst enemy had been disposed of and a man might breathe freely once more. The crowd could think of nothing to talk about that whole morning but that B. J. "beast" and his ruin.

They found something, however, before many more minutes passed. Bull chanced to glance over his shoulder in the direction of the camp.

"Hello!" he said. "Here comes Fischer."

"Good-afternoon, Mr. Fischer," said Bull.

"Good-afternoon," responded the officer, with obvious stiffness; and then there was an awkward silence, during which he surveyed them in silence.

"Mr. Harris," he said, at last, "I'd like to speak to you for a moment; and Mr. Murray, and you, too, Mr. Vance."

The three stepped out of the group with alacrity, and followed Fischer over to a seat nearby, while the rest of the gang stood and stared in surprise, speculating as to what this could possibly mean.

The three with the officer were finding out in a hurry.

"I am told," began the latter, gazing at them, with majestic sternness, "that you three are engaged in skinning a certain plebe—"

"Why, Mr. Fischer!" cried the three, in obvious surprise.

"Don't interrupt me!" thundered the captain in a voice that made them quake, and that reached the others and made them quake, too.

"Don't interrupt me! I know what I am talking about. I was a yearling once myself, and I'm a cadet still, and there's not the least use trying to pull the wool over my eyes. I know there never yet was a plebe who got fifty demerits in one day and deserved them."

The captain did not fail to notice here that the trio flushed and looked uncomfortable.

"You all know, I believe," he continued, "just exactly what I think of you. I've never hesitated to say it. Now, I want you to understand in the first place that I know of this contemptible trick, and that also I know the plebe, who's worth more than a dozen of you; and that if he gets a demerit from any one of you again I'll make you pay for it as sure as I'm alive. Just remember it, that's all!"

And with this, the indignant captain turned upon his heel, and strode off, leaving the yearlings as if a bombshell had landed in their midst.

"Fischer's a confounded fool!" Bull Harris broke out at last.

"Just what he is!" cried the Baby. "I'd like to knock him over."

And after that there was silence again, broken only by the roll of a drum that meant dinner.

"Well," was Bull's final word, as the crowd set out for camp, "it's unfortunate, I must say. But it won't make the least bit of difference. Mallory'll get his demerits sure as he's alive, and Fischer's interference won't matter in the least."

"That's what!" cried the rest of them.

CHAPTER XXV

A SWIMMING MATCH

The manner in which the cadets dine has not as yet been described in these pages; perhaps here is just as good a place as any to picture the historic mess hall where Lee and Grant and Sherman once dined, and toward which on that Saturday afternoon were marching not only the group we have just left, but also the object of all their dislike, the B. J. plebe who fell in behind the cadets as the battalion swung past barracks.

The cadets march to mess hall; they march to every place they go as a company. The building itself is just south of the "Academic" and barracks; it is built of gray stone, and forcibly reminds the candid observer of a jail. They tell stories at West Point of credulous candidates who have "swallowed" that, and believed that the cadet battalion was composed of disobedient cadets, about to be locked up in confinement.

There is a flight of iron steps in the center, and at the foot of these steps, three times every day, the battalion breaks ranks and dissolves into a mob of actively bounding figures. Upon entering, the cadets do not take seats, but stand behind their chairs, and await the order, "Company A, take seats!" "Company B, take seats!" and so on. The plebes, who, up to this time, are still a separate company, come last, as usual; they are seated by themselves, at one side of the dining-room.

The tables seat twenty-two persons, ten on a side, and one at each end. The cadets are placed according to rank, and they always sit in the same seats. The tables are divided down the center by an imaginary line, each part being a "table"; first class men sit near the head, and so on down to the plebes, who find themselves at the center (that is, after they have moved into camp, and been "sized" and assigned to companies; before that they are "beasts," herded apart, as has been said).

The dinner is upon the table when the cadets enter; the

corporals are charged with the duty of carving, and the luckless plebe is expected to help everybody to water upon demand, and eats nothing until that duty has been attended to. After the meal, for which half an hour is allowed, the command, "Company A, rise!" and so on, is the signal to leave the table and fall into line again on the street outside. This, however, does not take place until a lynx-eyed "tac" has gone the rounds, making notes—"So-and-so, too much butter on plate." "Somebody else, napkin not properly folded," and so on. This ceremony over, the battalion marches back to camp, a good half mile, in the broiling sun or pouring rain, as the case may be.

That Saturday afternoon being a hot one, and a holiday, our friends of the last chapter, Bull Harris and his gang, sought out an occupation in which fully half the cadets at the post chanced to agree; they went in swimming, a diversion which the superintendent sees fit to allow. "Gee's Point," on the Hudson, is within the government property, and thither the cadets gather whenever the weather is suitable.

That particular party included Bull and Baby (who didn't swim, but liked to watch Bull), Gus Murray, Vance and the rest of their retainers. And, on the way, they passed the time by discussing their one favorite topic, their recent triumph over "that B. J. beast." There was a new phase of the question they had to speculate upon now, and that was what the "beast" could possibly have done to move to such unholy wrath so important a personage as the senior captain of the Battalion. Also, they were interested in trying to think up a method by which those extra demerits might be speedily given without incurring the wrath of that officer. Though each one of the yearlings was ready, even anxious, to explain that he wasn't the least bit afraid of him.

"I tell you," declared Bull, "he couldn't prove anything against us if he tried. It's all one great bluff of Fischer's, and he's a fool to act as he did."

"I'd a good mind to tell him as much!" assented Baby.

"It won't make any difference," put in Murray, "we'll soak the plebe, anyhow. We can easily give him five demerits in short order, and without attracting any attention, either."

"He's out, just as sure as he's alive!" laughed Bull. "We wouldn't need to do a thing more."

"Exactly!" cried the echo. "Not a thing!"

"All the same," continued the other, "I wish we could get up a scheme to get him in disgrace, so as to clinch it. I wish we could—"

Just here Bull was interrupted by a sudden exclamation from Murray. Murray had brought his hand against his knee with a whack, and there was a look of inspiration upon his face.

"Great Cæsar!" he cried, "I've got it!"

"Got it! What?"

"A scheme! A scheme to do him!"

"What is it?"

"Write him a letter, or something—get him to leave barracks at night—have a sentry catch him beyond limits, or else we'll report him absent! Oh, say!"

The crowd were staring at each other in amazement, a look of delight spreading over their faces, as the full possibilities of this same inspiration dawned upon them.

"By the lord!" cried Bull, at last. "Court-martial him! That's the ticket!"

"Shake on it!" responded Murray.

In half a minute the gang had sworn to put that plan into execution within the space of twenty-four hours. And after that they hurried on down to the point to go in swimming.

"Speak of angels," remarked Murray, "and they flap their wings. There's the confounded plebe now."

"Of angels!" sneered Vance. "Of devils, you mean."

"By George!" muttered Bull. "You can't phaze that fellow. I thought he'd be up in barracks, moping, to-day!"

"Probably wants to put up a bluff as if he don't care," was the clever suggestion of the Baby. "I bet he's sore as anything!"

"I told him I'd make him the sickest plebe in the place," growled Bull, "and I'll bet he is, too."

The yearling would have won his bet; there was probably no sadder man in West Point than Mark Mallory just then, even though he did not choose to let his enemies know it.

"Look at him dive!" sneered Baby, watching him with a malignant frown. "He wants to show off."

"Pretty good dive," commented a bystander, who was somewhat more disinterested.

"Good, your grandmother!" cried the other. "Why, I could beat that myself if I knew how to swim!"

And then he wondered why the crowd laughed.

"Come on, let's go in ourselves," put in Bull, anxious to end his small friend's discomfort. "Hurry up, there!"

The crowd had turned away, to follow their leader in his suggestion; they were by no means anxious to swell the number of those who had gathered for the obvious purpose of watching Mark Mallory's feats as a swimmer. In fact, they couldn't see why anybody should want to watch a B. J. beast, and a "beast" who had only a day or two more to stay, at that.

Just then, however, a cry from the crowd attracted their attention, and made them turn hastily again.

"A race! A race!"

And Bull Harris cried out with vexation, as he wheeled and took in the situation.

"By the Lord!" he cried. "Did you ever hear of such a B. J. trick in your life? The confounded plebe is going to race with Fischer!"

CHAPTER XXVI

THE FINISH OF A RACE

So it was; certain of the cadets, being piqued at the evident superiority which that B. J. Mallory (his usual title by this time) had displayed in the water, had requested their captain to take him down. The "captain" had good-naturedly declared that he was willing to try; and the shout that attracted Bull's attention was caused by the plebe's ready assent to the proposition for an impromptu race.

"Fischer ought to be ashamed of himself, to have anything to do with him!" was Bull Harris' angry verdict. "I almost hope the plebe beats him."

"I don't!" vowed Murray, emphatically. "Let's hurry up, and see it."

The latter speaker suited the action to the word; Bull followed, growling surlily.

"Look at that gang of plebes!" he muttered. "They're the ones who helped Mallory take away the fellow we were hazing; they think they're right in it, now."

"Yes," chimed in Baby. "And see that fellow, Texas, making a fool of himself."

"That fellow Texas" was "making a fool of himself" by dancing about in wild excitement, and raising a series of cowboy whoops in behalf of his friend, and of plebes in general.

"There they are, ready to go!" cried Murray, betraying some excitement.

"I wish the confounded plebe'd never come up again!" growled Bull, in return, striving hard to appear indifferent.

"I bet Fischer'll do him!" exclaimed the Baby. "He swims like a fish. Say, they're going to race to that tree way down the river. Golly, but that's a long swim!"

"Long nothing!" sneered Vance. "I could swim that a dozen times. But, say, they'll finish in the rain; look at that thunderstorm coming!"

In response to this last remark, the crowd cast their eyes in the direction indicated. They found that the prediction seemed likely to be fulfilled. To the north, up the Hudson, dense, black clouds already obscured the sky, and a strong, fresh breeze, that smelled of rain, was springing up from thence, and making the swimmers shiver apprehensively.

The preparation for the race went on, however; nobody cared for the storm.

"Gee whiz!" cried the Baby, in excitement. "Won't it be exciting! I don't mind the rain. I'm going to run down along the shore, and watch it! Hooray!"

"Rats!" growled Bull, angrily. "I don't care about any old race. I'm going to keep dry, let me tell you!"

Even the damper of his idol's displeasure could not change Master Edwards' mind, however; he and nearly the whole crowd with him made a dash down the shore for a vantage point to see the finish.

"There! They're off!"

The cry came a moment later, as the two lightly-clad figures stepped to the mark from which they were to start.

They were about of one size, magnificently proportioned, both of them, and the race bid fair to be a close one.

"Ready?" called the starter, in a voice that rang down the shore.

"Yes," responded Mark, and at the same moment a heavy cloud swept under the sun, and the air grew dark and chilly. The wind increased to a gale, blowing the spray before it; and then— —

"Go!" called the starter.

The two dived as one figure; both took the water clean and low, with no perceptible splash; two heads appeared a moment later, forging ahead side by side; a cheer from the cadets arose, that drowned, for a moment, the roars of the storm; and the race was on.

It is remarkable how closely nature follows a rule in her most perfect work; here were two figures, built by her a thousand miles apart, racing there, and each striving with might and main, yet the sum total of the energy that each was able to expend so nearly alike that yard by yard they struggled on, without an inch of difference between them.

"Fischer! Fischer!" rose the shouts of the cadets.

"Mallory! Mallory!" roared the excited plebes, backed up by an occasional "Wow!" in the stentorian tones of the mighty Texan, who, by this time, was on the verge of epilepsy.

Onward went the two heads, still side by side, seeming to creep through the water at a snail's pace to the excited partisans on the shore. But it was no snail's pace to the two in the water; each was struggling in grim earnestness, putting into every stroke all the power that was in him. Neither looked at the other; but each could tell, from the cries of the cadets, that his opponent was pressing him closely.

Nearer and nearer they came to the far distant goal; higher and higher rose the shouts:

"Fischer! Fischer!" "Mallory! Mallory!" "He's got him!" "No." "Hooray!"

"Gee! but it is exciting," screamed Baby. "Go it, Fischer! Do him!"

"And I wish that confounded 'beast' was in Hades!" snarled Bull, whose hatred of Mark was deeper, and more malignant than that of his friend.

"I believe I could kill him!"

During all this excitement the storm had been sweeping rapidly up, its majesty unnoticed in the excitement of the race. Far up the Hudson could be seen a driving cloud of rain; and the wind had risen to a hurricane, while the air grew dark and chill.

The race was at its most exciting stage—the finish, and the cadets were dancing about, half in a frenzy, yelling incoherently, at the two still struggling lads, when some one, nobody knew just who, chanced to glance for one brief instant up the river. A moment later a cry was heard that brought the race to a startling and unexpected close.

"Look! look! The sailboat!"

The cry sounded even above the roar of the storm and the shouts of the crowd. The cadets turned in alarm and gazed up the river. What they saw made them forget that such a thing as a race ever existed.

Right in the teeth of the wind, in the center of the river, was a small catboat, driven downstream, before the gale, with the speed of a locomotive. In the boat was one person, and the person was a girl. She sat in the stern, waving her hands in helpless terror, and even as the spectators stared, the boat gibed with terrific violence, and a volume of water poured in over the gunwale.

The crowd was thrown into confusion; a babel of excited voices arose, and the race was forgotten in an instant.

The racers were not slow to notice it; both of them turned to gaze behind them, and to take in the situation.

"Help! Help!" called a faint voice from the distant sailboat.

Help! Who was there to help? There was not a boat in sight; the cadets were running up and down in confusion, hunting for one in vain. They were like a nest of frightened ants, without a leader, skurrying this way and that, and only contributing to the general alarm. The girl herself could do nothing, and so it seemed as if help were far away, indeed.

There was one person in the crowd, however, who kept his head in the midst of all that confusion. And the person was Mark. Exhausted though he was by his desperate swim, he did not hesitate an instant. Before the amazed cadet captain at his side could half comprehend his intention, he turned quickly in the water, and, with one powerful stroke, shot away toward the center of the stream.

The cadets on the shore scarcely knew whether to cry out in horror, or to cheer the act they saw. They caught one more glimpse of the catboat as it raced ahead before the gale; they saw the gallant plebe struggling in the water.

And then the storm struck them in its fury. A blinding sheet of driving rain, that darkened the air and drove against the river, and rose again in clouds of spray; a gale that lashed the water into fury; and darkness that shut out the river, and the boat, and the swimmer, and left nothing but a humbled group of shivering cadets.

CHAPTER XXVII

WHAT MARK DID

The surprise of the helpless watchers on the shore precludes description. They knew that out upon that seething river a tragedy was being enacted; but the driving rain made a wall about them—they could not aid, they could not even see. They stood about in groups, and whispered, and listened, and strained their eyes to pierce the mist.

Mark's friends were wild with alarm; and his enemies—who can describe their feelings?

A man has said that it is a terrible thing to die with a wrong upon one's soul; but that it is agony to see another die whom you have wronged, to know that your act can never be atoned for now. That there is one unpardonable sin to your account on the records of eternity. That was how the yearlings felt; and even Bull Harris, ruffian though he was, trembled slightly about the lips.

The storm itself was one of those which come but seldom. Nature's mighty forces flung loose in one giant cataclysm. It came from the north, and it had a full sweep down the valley of the Hudson, pent in and focused to one point by the mountains on each side. It tore the trees from the tops as it came; it struck the river with a swish, and beat the water into foam. It flung the raindrops in gusts against it, and caught them up in spray and whirled them on; and this, to the echoing crashes of the thunder and the dull, lurid gleam of the lightning that played in the rear.

One is silent at such times at that; the frightened cadets on the shore would probably have stood in groups and trembled, and done nothing through it all, had it not been for a cry that aroused them. Some one, sharper eyed than the rest, espied a figure struggling in the water near the shore. There was a rush for the spot, and strong arms drew the swimmer in. It was Captain Fischer, breathless and exhausted from the race.

He lay on the bank, panting for breath for a minute, and then raised himself upon his arms.

"Where's Mallory?" he cried, his voice sounding faint and distant in the roar of the storm.

"Out there," responded somebody, pointing.

"W-why don't somebody go help him?" gasped the other. "He'll drown!"

"Don't know where to go to," answered the first speaker, shaking his head.

Fischer sank back, too exhausted, himself, to move.

"He'll drown! He'll drown!" he muttered. "He is tired to death from the race."

And after that there was another anxious wait, every one hesitating, wondering if there were any use venturing into the tossing water.

The storm was one that came in gusts; its first minute's fury past, there was a brief let up in its violence, and the darkness that the black clouds had brought with them yielded to the daylight for a while. During that time those on the shore got one brief glimpse of a startling panorama.

The boat was sighted first, still skimming along before the gale, but obviously laboring with the water she had shipped. The frightened occupant was still in the stern, clinging to the gunwale with terror. There was a shout raised when the boat was noticed, and all eyes were bent upon it anxiously. Then some one, chancing a glance down the river below, caught a glimpse of a moving head.

"There's Mallory!" he cried. "Hooray!"

There was Mallory, and Mallory was swimming desperately, as the crowd could dimly see. For the boat he was aiming at was just a little farther out in the stream than he, and bearing swiftly down upon him. Whatever happened must happen with startling rapidity, and the crowd knew it, and forebore to shout—almost to breathe.

The boat plunged on; the swimmer fairly leaped through the waves. Nearer it came, nearer—up to him—past him! No! For, as it seemed, the bow must cleave his body, the body was seen to leap forward with it. He had caught the boat! And a wild cheer burst from the spectators.

"He's safe! He's safe!"

But the cheer, as it died out, seemed to catch in their throats, and to change into a gasp of suspense, and then of horror.

Mallory had clung to the bow for a moment, as if too exhausted to move. His body, half submerged, had cut a white furrow in the water, drawn on by the plunging boat. Then the girl, in an evil moment, released her hold and sprang forward to help him. She caught his arm, and he flung himself upon the boat.

And then came the crash.

Leaning to one side, with the sudden weight, the boat half turned, and then gibed with terrific violence. The great boom swung around like a giant club, driven by the pressure of the wind upon the vast surface of the sail. The watchers gave a half-suppressed gasp, Mallory was seen to put out his arm, and the next instant the blow was struck.

It hit the girl with a crash that those on shore thought they heard; it flung her far out into the water, and almost at the same instant Mallory was seen to leap out in a low, quick dive. Then, as if the scene was over, and the book shut, the rain burst out again in its fury, and the darkness of the raging storm shut it all out.

This time there could be no mistaking duty; the cadets knew now where the struggling pair were, and they had no reason to hesitate. First to move was one of a group of six anxious plebes, who had been waiting in agony; it was Texas, and the spectators saw him plunge into the water and vanish in the driving rain. Then more of that crowd followed him; Fischer, too, sprang up, exhausted though he was, and in the end there were at least a dozen sturdy lads swimming with all their might toward the spot where Mallory had been seen to leap.

They were destined, however, to do but little good; so we shall stay by those upon the shore.

The weakening of Bull Harris' followers has been mentioned; it increased as the plebe's self-sacrificing daring was shown.

"He certainly is spunky," one of the crowd ventured to mutter, as he shivered and watched. "I hope he gets ashore."

And Bull turned upon him with a savage oath.

"You fool!" he cried. "You confounded fool! If he does, I could kill him! Kill him! Do you hear me?"

There are some natures like that. Have you read the tale of Macauley's?—

>*"How brave Horatius held the bridge*
>*In the good old days of yore."*

There was just such a hero then battling with the waves as now—

>*"Curse him!" cried false Sextus.*
>*"Will not the villain drown?"*

And on the other hand—

>*"Heaven help him," quoth Spurius Laritus, "*
>*And bring him safe to shore!*
>*For such a gallant feat of arms*
>*Has ne'er been seen before."*

There were few of Bull's crowd as hardened in their hatred as was he; Murray was one, and the sallow Vance another. Baby Edwards followed suit, of course. But, as for the rest of them, they were thinking.

"I don't care!" vowed one. "I'm sorry we've got him fired."

"Do you mean," demanded Bull, in amazement, "that you're not going to keep the promise you made a while ago?"

"That's what I do!" declared the other, sturdily. "I think he deserves to stay!"

And Bull turned away in alarm and disgust.

"Fools!" he muttered to himself. "Fools!" and gritted his teeth in rage. "I hope he's never seen again."

It seemed as if that might happen; the cadets during all this time had been standing out in the driving rain, striving to pierce the darkness of the storm. From the river came an occasional shout from some one of the rescue party; but no word from the plebe or the girl.

Once the watchers caught sight of a figure swimming in; it

proved to be Fischer once more. The cadets had rushed toward him with sudden hope, but he shook his head, sadly.

"Couldn't—couldn't find him," he panted, shaking the water from his hair and shielding his face from the driving rain. "I was too tired to stay long."

The storm swept by in a very short while. Violence such as that cannot last long in anything. While the anxious cadets raced up and down the shore, each striving to catch a glimpse of Mallory, the dark clouds sailed past and the rain settled into an ordinary drizzle. The surface of the white-capped river became visible then, and gradually the heads of the swimmers came into view.

"There's Billy Williams!" was the cry. "And that's Texas, way over there. Here's Parson Stanard! And Jones!"

And so on it went, but no Mallory. Those on the shore could not see him and those in the river had no better luck. Most of them had begun to give up in despair, when the long-expected cry did come. For Mark was not dead by a long shot.

A shout came from a solitary straggler far down the stream, and the straggler was seen to plunge into the water. Those on the shore made a wild dash for the spot and those in the water struck out for the shore so as to join them. And louder at last swelled the glad cry.

"Here he is! Hooray!"

The plebe was about a hundred yards from the shore, and swimming weakly; the girl, still unconscious, was floating upon her back—and her rescuer, holding her by the arms—was slowly towing her toward the shore.

A dozen swam out to aid him as soon as he was seen; strong arms lifted the girl and bore her high upon the bank, others supporting the half-fainting plebe to a seat.

"Is she dead?" was Mark's first thought, as soon as he could speak at all.

"I don't know," said Fischer, chafing the girl's hands and watching for the least sign of life. "Somebody hustle up for the doctor there! Quick!"

Several of the cadets set out for the hospital at a run; and the rest gathered about the two and offered what help they could.

"It's Judge Fuller's daughter," said Fischer, who was busily dosing the unconscious figure with a flask of reddish liquid surreptitiously produced by one of the cadets.

"Do you know her?" inquired Mark, in surprise.

"Know her!" echoed half the bystanders at once. "Why, she lives just across the river!"

"That's an ugly looking wound on the head there," continued Fischer, bending over the prostrate form. "Gosh! but that boom must have struck her. And here, Mallory," he added, "you'd best take a taste of this brandy. You look about dead yourself."

"No, I thank you," responded Mark, smiling weakly. "I'm all right. Only I'm glad it's all over and— —"

Mark got no farther; as if to mock his words came a cry that made the crowd whirl about and look toward the river in alarm.

"Help! Help!"

"By George!" cried Fischer, "it's one of the fellows!"

"It's Alan!" shouted Mark. "Alan Dewey!"

And before any one could divine his intention he sprang up and made a dash for the river. For Mark knew how Dewey had come there; he had swum out, cripple though he was, to hunt for him; and with his one well arm, poor gallant Dewey was finding trouble in getting back.

Mark had been quick, but Fischer was a bit too quick for him and seized him by the arm.

"Come back here!" he commanded, sternly. "And don't be a fool. You're near dead. Some of you fellows swim out and tow that plebe in."

Half a dozen had started without being asked; and Mark's overzealous friend was grabbed by the hair and arms and feet and rushed in in great style. He came up smiling as usual.

"Got out too far, b'gee!" he began. "Very foolish of me! Reminds me of a story I once heard— — Oh, say!"

This last explanation came as the speaker caught sight of the figure of the young girl; and his face lost its smile on the instant.

"She's alive, isn't she?" he cried.

"Don't know," said Fischer. "Here comes the doctor now."

"Well, she certainly is a beautiful girl!" responded Dewey, shaking his head. "B'gee, we don't want that kind to die!"

The doctor was coming on a run; and a minute later he was kneeling beside the young girl's body.

"Jove!" he muttered. "Almost a fractured skull! No, she's alive! See here, who got her out?"

"Mr. Mallory," responded the captain, turning toward where Mark had sat. And then he gave vent to a startled exclamation.

"Good heavens! He's fainted! What's the matter?"

"Fainted?" echoed the surgeon, as he noticed the young man's white lips and bloodless cheek. "Fainted! I should say so! Why, he's almost as near dead as she! We must take him to the hospital."

CHAPTER XXVIII

MARK MEETS THE SUPERINTENDENT

"Yes, colonel, the lad is a hero, and I want to tell him so, too!"

The speaker was a tall, gray-haired gentleman, and he whacked his cane on the floor for emphasis as he spoke.

"It was a splendid act, sir, splendid!" he continued. "And I want to thank Mark Mallory for it right here in your office."

The man he addressed wore the uniform of the United States army; he was Colonel Harvey, the superintendent of the West Point Academy.

"I shall be most happy to have you do so," he replied, smiling at this visitor's enthusiasm. "You have certainly," he added, "much to thank the young man for."

"Much!" echoed the other. "Much! Why, my dear sir, if that daughter of mine had been drowned I believe it would have killed me. She is my only child, and, if I do say it myself, sir, the sweetest girl that ever lived."

"Wasn't it rather reckless, judge," inquired the other, "for you to allow her to go sailing alone?"

"She is used to the boat," responded Judge Fuller, "but no one on earth could have handled it in such a gale. I do not remember to have seen such a one in all the time I have lived up here."

"Nor I, either," said the superintendent. "It was so dark that I could scarcely see across the parade ground. It is almost miraculous that Mallory should have succeeded in finding the boat as he did."

"Tell me about it," put in the other. "I have not been able to get a consistent account yet."

"Cadet Captain Fischer told me," responded the colonel. "It seems that he and Mallory were just at the finish of a swimming race when the storm broke. They caught sight of the boat with your daughter in it coming down stream. The plebe turned, exhausted though he was, and headed for it. It got so dark then that those on shore could scarcely see; but the lad managed to catch the boat as it passed and climbed aboard. Just then the boom swung round and flung the girl into the water. Mallory dived again at once— —"

"Splendid!" interrupted the other.

"And swam ashore with her."

"And then fainted, they say," the judge added.

"Yes," said Colonel Harvey. "Dr. Grimes told me that it was one of the worst cases of exhaustion he had ever seen. But the lad is doing well now; he appears to be a very vigorous youngster—and I've an idea several of the yearlings found that out to their discomfort. The doctor told me that he thought he would be out this morning; the accident was only two days ago."

"That is fortunate," responded the other. "The boy is too good to lose."

"He appears to be a remarkable lad generally," continued the superintendent. "I have heard several tales about him. Some of the stories came to me 'unofficially,' as we call it, and I don't believe Mallory would rest easily if he thought I knew of them. Young Fischer, who's a splendid man himself, I'll tell you, informed me yesterday that the plebe had earned his admission fee by bringing help to a wrecked train and telegraphing the account to a New York paper."

"I heard he had been in some trouble about demerits," put in Judge Fuller.

"In very serious trouble. I had to take a very radical step to get him out of it. Every once in a while I find that some new cadet is being 'skinned,' as the cadets call it, demerited unfairly. I always punish severely when I find that out. In this case, though, I had no proof; Mallory would say nothing, though he was within five demerits of expulsion. So I decided to end the whole matter by declaring a new rule I've been contemplating for some time. I've found that new cadets get too many demerits during the first few weeks, before they learn the rules thoroughly. So I've decided that in future no demerits shall be given for the first three weeks, and that delinquencies shall be punished by extra hours and other penalties. That let Mallory out of his trouble, you see."

"A very clever scheme!" laughed the other. "Very clever!"

It may be of interest to notice that Colonel Harvey's rule has been in effect ever since.

There was silence of a few moments after that, during which Judge Fuller tapped the floor with his cane reflectively.

"You promised to let me see this Mallory," he said, suddenly. "I'm ready now."

By way of answer, the superintendent rang a bell upon his desk.

"Go over to the hospital," he said to the orderly who appeared in the doorway, "and find out if Cadet Mallory is able to be about. If he is, bring him here at once."

The boy disappeared and the colonel turned to his visitor and smiled.

"Is that satisfactory?" he inquired.

"Very!" responded the other. "And I only wish that you could send for my daughter to come over, too. I hope those surgeons are taking care of her."

"As much as if she were their own," answered the colonel. "I cannot tell you how glad I was to learn that she is beyond danger."

"It is God's mercy," said the other, with feeling. "She could not have had a much narrower escape."

And after that neither said anything until a knock at the door signaled the arrival of the orderly.

"Come in," called the superintendent, and two figures stepped into the room. One was the messenger, and the other was Mark.

"This," said the superintendent after a moment's pause, "is Cadet Mallory."

And Cadet Mallory it was. The same old Mark, only paler and more weak just then.

Judge Fuller rose and bowed gravely.

"Sit down," said he, "you are not strong enough to stand."

And after that no one said anything for fully a minute; the last speaker resumed his seat and fell to studying Mark's face in silence. And Mark waited respectfully for him to begin.

"My name," said he at last, "is Fuller."

"Judge Fuller?" inquired Mark.

"Yes. And Grace Fuller is my daughter."

After that there was silence again, broken suddenly by the excitable old gentleman dropping his cane, springing up from his chair, and striding over toward the lad.

"I want to shake hands with you, sir! I want to shake hands with you!" he cried.

Mark was somewhat taken aback; but he arose and did as he was asked.

"And now," said the judge, "I guess that's all—sit down, sir, sit down; you've little strength left, I can see. I want to thank you, sir, for being the finest lad I've met for a long time. And when my daughter gets well—which she will, thank the Lord—I'll be very glad to have you call on us, or else to let us call on you—seeing that we live beyond cadet limits. And if ever you get into trouble, here or anywhere, just come and see me about it, and I'll be much obliged to you. And that's all."

Having said which, the old gentleman stalked across the room once more, picked up his hat and cane, and made for the door.

"Good-day, sir," he said. "I'm going around now to see my daughter. Good-day, and God bless you."

After which the door was shut.

It was several minutes after that before Colonel Harvey said anything.

"You have made a powerful friend, my boy," he remarked, smiling at the recollection of the old gentleman's strange speech. "And you have brought honor upon the academy. I am proud of you—proud to have you here."

"Thank you, sir," said Mark, simply.

"All I have to say besides that," added the officer, "is to watch out that you stay. Don't get any more demerits."

"I'll try not, sir."

"Do. And I guess you had best go and join your company now if the doctor thinks you're able. Something is happening to-day which always interests new cadets. I bid you good-morning, Mr. Mallory."

And Mark went out of that office and crossed the street to barracks feeling as if he were walking on air.

CHAPTER XXIX

THE SEVEN IN SESSION

It is fun indeed to be a hero, to know that every one you pass is gazing at you with admiration. Or if one cannot do anything heroic, let him even do something that will bring him notoriety, and then—

"As he walks along the Boulevard,
With an independent air."

he may be able to appreciate the afore-mentioned sensation.

There was no boulevard at West Point, but the area in barracks served the purpose, and Mark could not help noticing that as he went the yearlings were gazing enviously at him, and the plebes with undisguised admiration. He hurried upstairs to avoid that, and found that he had leaped, as the phrase has it, from the frying pan to the fire. For there were the other six of the "Seven Devils" ready to welcome him with a rush.

"Wow!" cried Texas. "Back again! Whoop!"

"Bless my soul, but I'm glad!" piped in the little round bubbly voice of "Indian." "Bless my soul!"

"Sit down. Sit down," cried "Parson" Stanard, reverently offering his beloved volume of "Dana's Geology" for a cushion.

"Sit down and let us look at you."

"Yes, b'gee!" chimed in Alan Dewey. "Yes, b'gee, let's look at you. Reminds me of a story I once heard, b'gee—pshaw, what's the use of trying to tell a good story with everybody trying to shout at once."

The excitement subsided after some five minutes more, and Mark was glad of it. With the true modesty natural to all high minds he felt that he would a great deal rather rescue a girl than be praised and made generally uncomfortable for it. So he shut his followers up as quickly as he could, which was not very quickly, for they had lots to say.

"How is the girl?" inquired Dewey, perceiving at last that Mark really meant what he said, and so, hastening to turn the conversation.

"She's doing very well now," said Mark.

"Always your luck!" growled Texas. "She's beautiful, and her father's a judge and got lots of money. Bet he runs off and marries her in a week. Oh, say, Mark, but you're lucky! You just ought to hear the plebes talk about you. I can't tell you how proud I am, man! Why——"

"Right back at it again!" interrupted Mark, laughing. "Right back again! Didn't I tell you to drop it? I know what I'll do——"

Here Mark arose from his seat.

"I hereby declare this a business meeting of the Seven Devils, and as chairman I call the meeting to order."

"What for?" cried the crowd.

"To consider plans for hazing," answered Mark. "I——"

"Wow!" roared Texas, wildly excited in an instant. "Goin' to haze somebody? Whoop!"

And Mark laughed silently to himself.

"I knew I'd make you drop that rescue business," he said. "And Mr. Powers, you will have the goodness to come to order and not to address the meeting until you are granted the floor. It is my purpose, if you will allow me to say a few words to the society—ahem!"

Mark said this with stern and pompous dignity and Texas subsided so suddenly that the rest could scarcely keep from laughing.

"But, seriously now, fellows," he said, after a moment's silence. "Let's leave all the past behind and consider what's before us. I really have something to say."

Having been thus enjoined, the meeting did come to order. The members settled themselves comfortably about the room as if expecting a long oration, and Mark continued, after a moment's thought.

"We really ought to make up our mind beforehand as to just exactly what we're going to do. I suppose you all know what's going to happen to-day."

"No!" cried the impulsive Texas. "I don't. What is it, anyhow?"

"We're to move to camp this afternoon," responded Mark.

"I know; but what's that got to do with it?"

"Lots. Several of the cadets have told me that there's always more hazing done on that one day than on all the rest put together. You see, we leave barracks and go up to live with the whole corps at the summer camp. And that night the yearlings always raise Cain with the plebes."

"Bully, b'gee!" chimed in Dewey, no less pleased with the prospect.

"So to-night is the decisive night," continued Mark. "And I leave it for the majority to decide just what we'll do about it. What do you say?"

Mark relapsed into silence, and there was a moment's pause, ended by the grave and classic Parson slowly rising to his feet. The Parson first laid his inevitable "Dana" upon the floor, then glanced about him with a pompous air and folded his long, bony arms. "Ahem!" he said, and then began:

"Gentlemen! I rise—ahem!—to put the case to you as I see it; I rise to emulate the example of the immortal Patrick Henry—to declare for liberty or death! Yea, by Zeus, or death!"

"Bully, b'gee!" chimed in Dewey, slapping his knee in approval and winking merrily at the crowd from behind the Parson's back.

"Gentlemen!" continued the Parson. "Once before we met in this same room and we did then make known our declaration of independence to the world. But there is one thing we have not yet done, and that we must do! Yea, by Zeus! I am a Bostonian—I may have told you that before—and I am proud of the deeds of my forefathers. They fought at Bunker Hill; and, gentlemen, we have that yet to do."

"Betcher life, b'gee!" cried Dewey, as the Parson gravely took his seat. Then the former arose and continued the discussion. "Not much of a hand for making a speech," he said, "as the deaf-mute remarked when he lost three fingers; but I've got something to say, and, b'gee, I'm going to say it. To-night is the critical night, and if we are meek and mild now, we'll be it for the whole summer. And I say we don't, b'gee, and that's all!"

With which brief, but pointed and characteristic summary of the situation, Alan sat down and Texas clapped his heels together and gave vent to a "Wow!" of approval.

"Anybody else got anything to say?" inquired Mark.

"Yes, bah Jove! I have, don't ye know."

This came from Mr. Chauncey Van Rensallear Mount-Bonsall. Chauncey wore a high collar and a London accent; he was by this time playfully known as "the man with a tutor and a hyphen," both of which luxuries it had been found he possessed. But Chauncey was no fool for all his mannerisms.

"Aw—yes," said he, "I have something to say, ye know. Those deuced yearlings will haze us more than any other plebes in the place. Beastly word, that, by the way. I hate to be called a plebe, ye know. There is blue blood in our family, bah Jove, and I'll guarantee there isn't one yearling in the place can show better. Why, my grandfather——"

"I call the gentleman to order," laughed Mark. "Hazing's the business on hand. Hazing, and not hancestors."

"I know," expostulated Chauncey, "but I hate to be called a plebe, ye know. As I was going to say, however, they'll haze us most. Mark has—aw—fooled them a dozen times, bah Jove! Texas chastised four of them. Parson, I'm told, chased half a dozen once. My friend Indian here got so deuced mad the other day that he nearly killed one, don't ye know. Dewey's worse, and as for me and my friend Sleepy here—aw—bah Jove!—--"

"You did better than all of us!" put in Mark.

Chauncey paused a moment to make a remark about "those deuced drills, ye know, which kept a fellah from ever having a clean collah, bah Jove!" And then he continued.

"I just wanted to say, ye know, that we were selected for the hazing to-night, and that we might as well do something desperate at once, bah Jove! that's what I think, and so does my friend Sleepy. Don't you, Sleepy?"

"I ain't a-thinkin' abaout it 't all," came a voice from the bed where Methusalem Zebediah Chilvers, the farmer, lay stretched out.

"Sleepy's too tired," laughed Mark. "It seems to be the

unanimous opinion of the crowd," he continued, after a moment's pause, "that we might just as well be bold. In other words, that we have no hazing."

"B'gee!" cried Dewey, springing to his feet, excitedly. "B'gee, I didn't say that! No, sir!"

"What did you say, then?" inquired Mark.

"I said that we shouldn't let them haze us, b'gee, and I meant it, too. I never said no hazing! Bet cher life, b'gee! I was just this moment going to make the motion that we carry the war into the enemy's country, that we upset West Point traditions for once and forever, and with a bang, too. In other words"—here the excitable youngster paused, so that his momentous idea might have due weight—"in other words, b'gee, that we haze the yearlings!"

There was an awed silence for a few moments to give that terrifically original proposition a chance to settle in the minds of the amazed "devils."

Texas was the first to act and he leaped across the room at a bound and seized "B'gee" by the hand.

"Wow!" he roared. "Whoop! Bully, b'gee!"

And in half a minute more the seven, including the timid Indian, had registered a solemn vow to do deeds of valor that would "make them ole cadets look crosseyed," as Texas put it.

They were going to haze the yearlings!

CHAPTER XXX

THE MOVE INTO CAMP

The new cadets at West Point are housed in barracks for two weeks after their admission. During this time "squad drill" is the daily rule, and the strangers learn to march and stand and face— everything a new soldier has to learn, with the exception of the manual of arms. After that they are adjudged fit to associate with the older cadets, and are marched up to "Camp McPherson." This usually takes place about the first day of July.

Our friends, the seven, had been measured for uniforms along with the rest of the plebe company during their first days in barracks. The fatigue uniforms had been given out that morning, to the great excitement of everybody, and now "cit" clothing, with all its fantastic variety of hats and coats of all colors, was stowed away in trunks "for good," and the plebes costumed uniformly in somber suits of gray, with short jackets and only a black seam down the trousers for ornament. Full dress uniforms, such as the old cadets up at camp were wearing, were yet things of the future.

That morning also the plebes had been "sized" for companies.

Of "companies" there are four, into which the battalion of some three hundred cadets is divided, "for purposes of instruction in infantry tactics, and in military police and discipline." (For purposes of "academic instruction," they are of course divided into the four classes: First, second, third, or "yearlings," and fourth, the "plebes".) The companies afore-mentioned are under the command of tactical officers. These latter report to the "commandant of cadets," who is, next to the superintendent, the highest ranking officer on the post.

The companies are designated A, B, C and D. A and D are flank companies, and to them the tallest cadets are assigned. B and C are center companies. Mark and Texas, and also the Parson and Sleepy, all of whom were above the average height, found themselves in A. The remainder of the Seven Devils managed to land in B; and the whole plebe class was ordered to pack up and be ready to move immediately after dinner.

The cadets are allowed to take only certain articles to camp; the rest, together with the cit's clothing, was stored in trunks and put away in the trunk room.

Right here at the start there was trouble for the members of our organization. Texas, it will be remembered, had a choice assortment of guns of all caliber, sixteen in number. These he had stored up the chimney of his room for safety. (The chimney is a favorite place of concealment for contraband articles at West Point). But there was no such place of concealment in camp; and no way of getting the guns there anyhow. There are no pockets in the cadets' uniforms except a small one for a watch. Money they are not allowed to carry, and their handkerchiefs are tucked in the breasts of their coats.

It was a difficult situation, for Texas, with true Texan cautiousness, vowed he'd never leave his guns behind.

"Why, look a yere, man," he cried. "I tell you, t'ain't safe now fo' a feller to go up thar 'thout anything to defend himself. You kain't tell what may happen!"

The Parson was in a similar quandary. His chimney contained a various assortment of chemicals, together with sundry geological specimens, including that now world-famous cyathophylloid coral which had been discovered "in a sandstone of Tertiary origin." And the Parson vowed that either that cyathophylloid went to camp or he stayed in barracks—yea, by Zeus!

There was no use arguing with them; Mark tried it in vain. Texas was obdurate and talked of holding up the crowd that dared to take those guns away; and the Parson said that he had kept a return ticket to Boston, his native town, a glorious city where science was encouraged and not repressed.

That was the state of affairs through dinner, and up to the moment when the cry, "New cadets turn out!" came from the area. By that time Texas had tied his guns in one of his shirts, and the Parson had variously distributed his fossils about his body until he was one bundle of lumps.

"If you people will congregate closely about me," he exclaimed, "I apprehend that the state of affairs will not be observed."

It was a curious assembly that "turned out"—a mass of

bundles, brooms and buckets, with a few staggering plebes underneath. They marched up to camp that way, too, and it was with audible sighs of relief that they dropped their burdens at the end.

A word of description of "Camp McPherson" may be of interest to those who have never visited West Point. It is important that the reader should be familiar with its appearance, for many of Mark's adventures were destined to happen there—some of them this very same night.

The camp is half a mile or so from barracks, just beyond the Cavalry Plain and very close to old Fort Clinton. The site is a pretty one, the white tents standing out against the green of the shade trees and the parapet of the fort.

The tents are arranged in four "company streets" and are about five feet apart. The tents have wooden platforms for floors and are large enough for four cadets each. A long wooden box painted green serves as the "locker"—it has no lock or key—and a wooden rod near the ridge pole serves as a wardrobe. And that is the sum total of the furniture.

The plebes made their way up the company streets and the cadet officers in charge, under the supervision of the "tacs," assigned them to their tents. Fortunately, plebes are allowed to select their own tent mates; it may readily be believed the four devils of A company went together. By good fortune the three remaining in B company, as was learned later, found one whole tent left over and so were spared the nuisance of a stranger in their midst—a fact which was especially gratifying to the exclusive Master Chauncey.

Having been assigned to their tents, the plebes were set to work under the brief instructions of a cadet corporal at the task of arranging their household effects. This is done with mathematical exactness. There is a place for everything, and a penalty for not keeping it there. Blankets, comforters, pillows, etc., go in a pile at one corner. A looking-glass hangs on the front tent pole; a water bucket is deposited on the front edge of the platform; candlesticks, candles, cleaning materials, etc., are kept in a cylindrical tin box at the foot of the rear tent pole; and so on it goes, through a hundred items or so. There are probably no more uniform things in all nature than the cadet tents in camp. The proverbial peas are not to be compared with them.

The amount of fear and trembling which was caused to those four friends of ours in a certain A company tent by the contraband goods of Texas and the Parson is difficult to imagine. The cadet corporal, lynx-eyed and vigilant, scarcely gave them a chance to hide anything. It was only by Mark's interposing his body before his friends that they managed to slide their precious cargoes in under the blankets, a temporary hiding place. And even when the articles were thus safely hidden, what must that officious yearling do but march over and rearrange the pile accurately, almost touching one of the revolvers, and making the four tremble and quake in their boots.

They managed the task without discovery, however, and went on with their work. And by the first drum beat for dress parade that afternoon, everything was done up in spick-and-span order, to the eye at any rate.

Dress parade was a formality in which the plebes took no part but that of interested spectators. They huddled together shyly in their newly occupied "plebe hotels" and watched the yearlings, all in spotless snowy uniforms, "fall in" on the company street outside. The yearlings were wild with delight and anticipation at having the strangers right among them at last, and they manifested great interest in the plebes, their dwellings, and in fact in everything about them. Advice and criticism, and all kinds of guying that can be imagined were poured upon the trembling lads' heads, and this continued in a volley until the second drum changed the merry crowd into a silent and motionless line of soldiers.

Mark could scarcely keep his excitable friend Texas from sallying out then and there to attack some of the more active members of this hilarious crowd. It was evident that, while no plebe escaped entirely, there was no plebe hotel in A company so much observed as their own. For the three B. J.-est plebes in the whole plebe class were known to be housed therein. Cadet Mallory, "professional hero," was urged in all seriousness to come out and rescue somebody on the spot, which oft-repeated request, together with other merry chaffing, he bore with a good-natured smile. Cadet Stanard was plagued with geological questions galore, among which the "cyathophylloid" occupied a prominent place. Cadet Powers was dared to come out and lasso a stray "tac," whose blue-uniformed figure was visible out on the parade ground. And Mr. Chilvers found the state of "craps" a point of great solicitude to all.

It was all stopped by the drum as has been mentioned; the company wheeled by fours and marched down the street, leaving the plebes to an hour of rest. But oh! those same yearlings were thinking. "Oh, won't we just soak 'em to-night!"

And, strange to say, the same thought was in the minds of seven particular plebes that stayed behind. For Mark had a plot by this time.

CHAPTER XXXI

"FIRST NIGHT"

Dress parade leaves but a few moments for supper, with no chance for "deviling." But when the battalion marched back from that meal and broke ranks, when the dusk of evening was coming on to make an effective screen, then was the time, thought the cadets. And so thought the plebes, too, as they came up the road a few minutes later, trembling with anticipation, most of them, and looking very solemn and somber in their dusky fatigue uniforms.

"First night of plebe camp," says a well-known military writer, "is a thing not soon to be forgotten, even in these days when pitchy darkness no longer surrounds the pranks of the yearlings, and when official vigilance and protection have replaced what seemed to be tacit encouragement and consent.

"Then—some years ago—it was no uncommon thing for a new cadet to be dragged out—'yanked'—and slid around camp on his dust-covered blanket twenty times a night, dumped into Fort Clinton ditch, tossed in a tent fly, half smothered in the folds of his canvas home, ridden on a tent pole or in a rickety wheelbarrow, smoked out by some vile, slow-burning pyrotechnic compound, robbed of rest and sleep at the very least after he had been alternately drilled and worked all the livelong day."

In Mark's time the effort to put a stop to the abuses mentioned had just been begun. Army officers had been put on duty at night; gas lamps had been placed along the sentry posts—precautions which are doubled nowadays, and with the risk of expulsion added besides. They have done away with the worst forms of hazing if not with the spirit.

The yearlings "had it in" for our four friends of company A that evening. In fact, scarcely had the plebes scattered to their tents when that particular plebe hotel was surrounded. The cadets had it all arranged beforehand, just what was to happen, and they expected to have no end of fun about it.

"Parson Stanard" was to be serenaded first; the crowd meant to surround him and "invite" him to read some learned extracts from his beloved "Dana." The Parson was to recount some of the nobler deeds of Boston's heroes, including himself; he was to display his learning by answering questions on every conceivable subject; he was to define and spell a list of the most outlandish words in every language known to the angels.

Texas was to show his skill and technique in hurling an imaginary lasso and firing an imaginary revolver from an imaginary galloping horse. He was to tell of the geography, topography, climate and resources of the Lone Star State; he was to recount the exploits of his "dad," "the Hon. Scrap Powers, sah, o' Hurricane Co.," and his uncle, the new Senator-elect. Mark was to give rules for rescuing damsels, saving expresses and ferryboats, etc. And Mr. Methusalem Zebediah Chilvers of Kansas was to state his favorite method of raising three-legged chickens and three-foot whiskers.

That was the delicious programme as finally agreed upon by the yearlings. And there was only one drawback met in the execution of it. The four plebes could not be found!

They weren't in their tent; they weren't in camp! Preposterous! The yearlings hunted, scarcely able to believe their eyes. The plebes, of course, had a perfect right to take a walk after supper if they chose. But the very idea of daring to do it on the first night in camp, when they knew that the yearlings would visit them and expect to be entertained! It was an unheard-of thing to do; but it was just what one would have expected of those B. J. beasts, so the yearlings grumbled, as they went off to other tents to engage other plebes in conversation and controversy.

But where were the four? No place in particular. They had simply joined the other three and had the impudence to disappear in the woods for a stroll until tattoo. They had come to the conclusion that it was better to do that than to stay and be "guyed," as they most certainly would be if they refused their tormentors' requests. And Mark had overruled Texas' vehement offer to stay and "do up the hull crowd," deciding that the cover of the night would be favorable to the sevens' hazing, and that until then they should make themselves scarce.

In the meantime there was high old sport in Camp McPherson. In response to the requests of the merry yearlings, some plebes were sitting out on the company streets and rowing desperate races at a 34-to-the-minute stroke with brooms for oars and air for water; some were playing imaginary hand-organs, while others sang songs to the tunes; some "beasts" were imitating every imaginable animal in a real "menagerie," and some were relating their personal history while trying to stand on their heads.

All this kind of hazing is good-natured and hurts no one physically, however much the loss of dignity may torment some sensitive souls. It is the only kind of hazing that remains to any great extent nowadays.

In the midst of such hilarity time passes very rapidly—to the yearlings, anyway. In almost no time tattoo had sounded; and then the companies lined up for the evening roll call, the seven dropping into line as silently as they had stolen off, deigning a word to no one in explanation of their strange conduct.

"That's what I call a pretty B. J. trick!" growled Cadet Harris. Bull had been looking forward with great glee to that evening's chance to ridicule Mark, with all his classmates to back him; it was a lost chance now, and Bull was angry in consequence.

Bull's cronies agreed with him as to the "B. J.-ness" of that trick. And they, along with a good many others, too, agreed that the trick ought not be allowed to succeed.

"We ought to haze him ten times as hard to-night to make up for it!" was the verdict.

And so it happened that the seven, by their action, brought down upon their heads all the hazing that was done after taps. This hazing, too, was by far the least pleasant, for it was attended to only by the more reckless members of the class, members who could not satisfy their taste for torture by making a helpless plebe sing songs, but must needs tumble him out of bed and ride him on a rail at midnight besides.

The fact, however, that all such members of the yearling class had decided to concentrate their torments upon him did not worry

Mark in the least. In fact, that was just what Mark had expected and prepared for.

And so there was destined to be fun that night.

"Now go to your tents, make down your bedding just as you were taught at barracks; do not remove your underclothing; hang up your uniforms where each man can get his own in an instant; put your shoes and caps where you can get them in the dark if need be; turn in and blow your candle out, before the drum strikes 'taps,' at ten. After that, not a sound! Get to sleep as soon as you can and be ready to form here at reveille."

So spoke Cadet Corporal Jasper; and then at the added command, "Break ranks, march!" the plebe company scattered, and with many a sigh of relief vanished as individuals in the various tents.

The corporal's last order, "be ready to form here at reveille," is a source of much worriment to the plebe. But the one before it, "get to sleep as soon as you can," is obeyed with the alacrity born of hours of drill and marching. Long before tattoo, which is the signal for "lights out," the majority of the members of the class were already dreaming. Perhaps they were not resting very easily, for most of them had a vague idea that there might be trouble that night; but they knew that lying awake would not stop it, and they were all too sleepy anyway.

The last closing ceremony of a West Point day in camp is the watchful "tac's" inspection. One of these officers goes the rounds with a dark lantern, flashing it into every tent and making sure that the four occupants are really in bed. (The "bed" consists of a board floor, and blankets.) Having attended to this duty, the tac likewise retires and Camp McPherson sinks into the slumbers of the night.

After that until five the next morning there is no one awake but the tireless sentries. A word about these. The camp is a military one and is never without guard from the moment the tents are stretched until the 29th of August, when the snowy canvas comes to the ground once more. The "guard tent" is at the western end of the camp, and is under the charge of the "corporal of the guard," a cadet. The sentries are cadets, too, and there are five of them, numbered—sentry No. 1 and so on. The ceremony each morning at which these sentries go on duty is called "guard-mounting." And during the next twenty-four hours these sentries are on duty two hours in every six—two hours on and then four off, making eight in the twenty-four.

These sentries being cadets themselves—and yearlings at present—hazing is not so difficult as it might seem. A sentry can easily arrange to have parties cross his beat without his seeing them; it is only when the sentry is not in the plot that the thing is dangerous.

The "tac"—Lieutenant Allen was his name—had made his rounds for the night, finding plebes and yearlings, too, all sleeping soundly, or apparently so. And after that there was nothing moving but the tramping sentinels, and the shadows of the trees in the moonlight as they fell on the shining tents—that is, there was nothing moving that was visible. The yearlings, plenty of them, were wide awake in their tents and preparing for their onslaught upon the sleeping plebes.

Sleeping? Perhaps, but certainly not all of them. Some of those plebes were as wide awake as the yearlings, and they were engaged in an occupation that would have taken the yearlings considerably by surprise if they had known it. There were seven of them in two tents, tents that were back to back and close together, one being in Company A and one in B.

They were very quiet about their work; for it was a risky business. Discovery would have meant the sentry's yelling for the corporal of the guard; meant that Lieutenant Allen would have leaped into his trousers and been out of his tent at the corporal's heels; meant a strict investigation, discovery, court-martial and dismissal. It was all right for yearlings to be out at night; but plebes—never!

It grew riskier still as a few minutes passed, for one of the B. J. beasts had the temerity to come out of his tent. He came very cautiously, it was true, worming his way along the ground silently, in true Indian—or Texas style. For Texas it was, that adventurous youth having vowed and declared that if he were not allowed to attend to this particular piece of mischief he would go out and hold up a sentry instead; the other three occupants were peering under the tent folds watching him anxiously as he crawled along.

As a fact, Texas' peril was not as great as was supposed, for the sentries had no means of telling if he was a yearling or not. The idea of a plebe's daring to break rules would not have occurred to them anyhow. Be that as it may, at any rate nobody interrupted the Seven Devils' plans. Cadet Powers made his way across the "street," deposited his burden, a glistening steel revolver some two feet long. And then he stole back and the crowd lay still in their tents and watched and waited.

They had not long to do that. Texas barely had time to crawl under the canvas and to mutter to his friends—for the hundredth time:

"Didn't I tell ye them air guns 'ud come in handy?"

At that very moment a sound of muffled laughter warned them that the moment had arrived.

"Just in time!" whispered Mark, seizing his friend by the hand and at the same time giving vent to a subdued chuckle. "Just in time. S-sh!"

The four, who lay side by side under the tent, could hear each other's hearts thumping then.

"Will it work? Will it work?" was the thought in the mind of every one of them.

CHAPTER XXXII

CONCLUSION

The yearlings were a merry party, about ten of them, and they were out for fun and all the fun that could be had. They were going to make it hot for certain B. J. plebes, and they meant to lose no time about it, either. They crept up the company street, laughing and talking in whispers, for fear they should arouse the tac. The sentries they did not care about, of course, for the sentries were pledged to "look the other way."

It was decided that the first thing to be done to those B. J. plebes was to "yank 'em." Yanking is a West Point invention. It means that the victim finds his blanket seized by one corner and torn from under him, hurling him to the ground. Many a plebe's nightmares are punctuated with just such periods as these.

It seems that a "yanking" was just what the four had prepared for. They had prepared for it by huddling up in one corner and rigging dummies to place in their beds. The dummies consisted of wash basins, buckets, etc., and it was calculated that when these dummies were yanked they would be far from dumb.

The yearlings stole up cautiously; they did not know they were watched. The breathless plebes saw their shadows on the tent walls, and knew just what was going on. They saw the figures line up at the back; they saw half a dozen pairs of hands gently raise the canvas, and get a good firm grip on the blankets. Then came a subdued "Now!" and then—well, things began to happen after that!

The yearlings "yanked" with all the power of their arms. The blankets gave way, and the result was a perfectly amazing clatter and crash. Have you ever heard half a dozen able-bodied dishwashers working at once?

Naturally the wildest panic resulted among the attacking party. They did not know what they had done, but they did know that they had done something desperate, and that they wished they hadn't. As the sound broke out on the still, night air they turned in alarm and made a wild dash for their tents.

Two of them raced down the company street at top speed; both of them suddenly struck an unexpected obstruction and were sent flying through the air. It was a string; and at one end of it was the Texas .44-caliber. The result was a bang that woke the camp with a jump. And then there was fun for fair.

The sentries knew then that every one was awake, including the "tac," and that they might just as well, therefore, "give the alarm." All five of them accordingly set up a wild shout for the corporal of the guard. This brought the young officer and Lieutenant Allen on the scene in no time. Also it brought from the land of dreams every cadet in the corps who had managed to sleep through the former racket. And nearly all of them rushed to their tent doors wondering what would happen next.

The seven meanwhile had been working like beavers. The instant the gun had gone off Texas, who held the string, had yanked it in and stowed it away with his other weapons, shaking with laughter in the meanwhile. The others had gone to work with a will; pitcher, basin, bucket, everything, had been hastily set in place; blankets had been relaid; and everything, in short, was put in order again, so that by the time that Lieutenant Allen got around to their tent—the officer had seized his lantern and set out on a hasty round to discover the jokers—he found four "scared" plebes, sitting up in beds, sleepily rubbing their eyes, and inquiring in anxiety:

"What's the matter?"

He didn't tell them, for he hadn't the remotest idea himself. And nobody told him; the yearlings couldn't have if they had wanted to.

Of course the lieutenant didn't care to stay awake all night, fruitlessly asking questions; so he went to bed. The sentries resumed their march, wondering meanwhile what on earth had led their classmates to make so much rumpus, and speculating as to whether it could possibly be true, what one cadet had suggested— that that wild and woolly Texan had tried to shoot some one who had hazed him. The rest of the cadets dropped off to sleep. And soon everybody was quiet again—that is, except the Seven Devils.

The Seven Devils had only just begun. They lay and waited until things were still, and then Mark gave the order, and the crowd rose as one man and stole softly out into the street. This included even the trembling Indian, who was muttering "Bless my soul!" at a great rate.

"I guess they're all asleep now," whispered Mark.

"What are you going to do?" inquired Indian.

"Yank 'em," responded Mark, briefly. "Come ahead."

Mark had seen that the yearlings came up boldly, which told him at once that the sentries were "fixed," and he calculated that just at the moment the moon being clouded, the sentries would not know yearlings from plebes. The only danger was that Lieutenant Allen might still be awake. It was risky, but then— —

"Do you see Bull Harris' tent?" Mark whispered. "It is the sixth from here. He and the Baby, with Vance and Murray, are in there. Now, then."

With trembling hearts the crowd crept down the street; this was their first venture as lawbreakers. They stole up behind the tent just as the yearlings had; they reached under the canvas and seized the blankets. And then came a sudden haul—and confusion and muttered yells from the inside, which told them that no dummies had been yanked this time.

The yearlings sprang up in wrath and gazed out; retreating footsteps and muffled laughter were all that remained, and they went back to bed in disgust. The plebes went, too, in high glee.

"And now," said Mark. "I guess we might as well go to sleep."

One does not like to leave this story without having a word to say about what the corps thought of the whole thing next morning. The "tac," of course, reported to his superior the night's alarm— "cause unknown," and that was the end of the matter officially. But the yearlings—phew!

The class compared notes right after reveille; and no one talked about anything else for the rest of that day. The cause of the rumpus made by the blankets was soon guessed; the two who had set off the gun were questioned, and that problem soon worked out also; that alone was bad enough! But the amazement when Bull and his tentmates turned up and declared that they—yearlings!—had been yanked, yes yanked, and by some measly plebes at that, there is no possibility of describing the indignation. Why, it meant that the class had been defied, that West Point had been overturned, that the world was coming to an end, and—what more could it possibly mean?

And through all the excitement the Seven just looked at each other—and winked:

"B. B. J.!" they said: "Just watch us!"

"It was great, b'gee!" said Dewey. "Hurrah for the plebes!"

"Hurrah!" was the answer, in a shout. "Hurrah!"

THE END